WATCHING
THE
ROSES

RED FOX  DEFINITIONS

WATCHING
THE
ROSES

ADÈLE GERAS

RED FOX DEFINITIONS

A Red Fox Book

Published by Random House Children's Books
20 Vauxhall Bridge Road, London SW1V 2SA

A division of The Random House Group Limited
London Melbourne Sydney Auckland
Johannesburg and agencies throughout the world

First published in Great Britain by Hamish Hamilton Ltd, 1991
Published by Red Fox, 2001

1 3 5 7 9 10 8 6 4 2

Printed and bound in Great Britain by
Bookmarque Ltd, Croydon, Surrey

Papers used by The Random House Group are natural, recyclable products
made from wood grown in sustainable forests. The manufacturing
processes conform to the environmental regulations
of the country of origin.

The Random House Group Limited Reg. No. 9540009

www.randomhouse.co.uk

ISBN 0 09 941723 5

For Frances Wilson

ONCE upon a time, I was a good girl and no trouble to anyone. Now, everyone is worried about me, although I don't think there's really anything that dreadful or strange about my behaviour. I do not want to speak, not at all, not to a single soul in the whole world, and therefore, I'm not speaking. I decided not to speak a week ago, and since then not one word has passed my lips. I stay in this room. I do not want to leave it. They bring me food on a tray and when they've gone, long after they've gone, I eat it. Then at least they don't have to worry about me starving to death. I truly don't want to worry anyone by what I'm doing, although already I can see signs that I have.

A week ago today was June 20th, and it was my eighteenth birthday party. It should have been a perfect day and it was spoiled, oh, horribly spoiled. They all try to get me to say something and I won't. In fact, every time I hear footsteps in the passage outside my door, I get on to the bed and arrange my hands over my body as if I were a medieval stone princess carved on an ancient tomb. I close my eyes. I become as stiff as I can and as still. As far as they're concerned, I won't speak and I won't move. I would like my mother to think that I am sleeping.

The doctor has been and examined me and shaken his head and gone, 'Tsk! tsk!' and whispered in a corner of my bedroom to my mother and father. I couldn't hear what he told them, but my mother (who quite often comes in to talk beside my bed, not really knowing whether I can hear her or not) said:

'You're exhausted, Alice. Nervously exhausted, that's what Dr Benyon says. He says we must let you rest and rest. First the exams, he says, and then . . . well, what happened at the party . . .' (she blinks very quickly in case I notice the tears in her eyes) 'you're simply worn out.'

That's a very good way of describing how I feel: worn out. As if I were a piece of cloth, or a sock or something that's been rubbed thinner and thinner until it's almost transparent. I am writing in an old notebook that must have belonged to my father when he was younger than I am now. I found it under a loose floorboard in my wardrobe. This was my father's room when he was a child. I'm quite used to the fact that my father is an expert on roses, and writes books about them and articles in magazines and newspapers telling people how best to take care of them, but now I can see the beginnings of this passion. In this notebook, he has copied down names of roses and a brief description of them, perhaps from an old catalogue. I like seeing what he wrote. I like the look of his young handwriting on the page and I feel as though he's provided a kind of decoration, an ornamental border for my own words. Perhaps, also, I will add something to what he has to say about the roses. I can see so many from this room.

When I was a very small child, my father used to take me for walks through the gardens. They seemed enormous then, laid out in elaborate patterns of flower-beds and terraces and arbours and lawns dotted with trees. The drive seemed to go on for ever, and the gates at the end of it rose up above my head as tall as cliffs. I couldn't reach the big ring that you had to twist to open them until I was seven years old. Now, although I can reach it easily enough, turning the ring to lift the latch would take all my strength. The gates usually stand open, but my father has closed them now. He closed them after all the guests had left the party.

As we walked about the garden, my father used to explain the roses to me: Damasks, Gallicas, Bourbons, Albas and the rest. I loved their names. So many of them were called after French-sounding ladies that I imagined them sweeping along the gravel paths in crinolines made of brocade and tall, powdered wigs: *Honorine de Brabant, Madame Lauriol de Barry, Comtesse de Murinais,* . . . there were scores of them, and I knew every one of them personally because my father did. He loved them and cared for them. I loved them and looked at them and inhaled their fragrance every summer, and felt saddened and betrayed when, year after year, having been so beautiful, they faded and grew brown along the edges of their petals and died.

'There'll be more roses next year,' my father used to tell me, and that was supposed to console me for the loss of these flowers, this particular beauty. In the end I grew suspicious of all the coloured glory and began instead to admire the winter skeletons of the plants. I liked the filigree pattern made by the dark stems, and the way the thorns stood out clearly, unhidden by any foliage or blooms.

Every evening, when I finish writing, I lock this notebook in a drawer of my desk, a secret drawer. Sometimes I imagine myself completely gone: dead, vanished, faded away, quite rubbed out, and then no one will think of looking in this hidden place for years and years, and these pages will just lie there, becoming yellow and dry like old petals. Someone will find them long after my death, and they won't know who I was or who anyone I've written about was, and they'll toss the whole notebook on the rubbish heap or put it on a bonfire.

Since the party, my dreams have been different. Before the night comes, I drift and slide into what I suppose are daydreams, because I know that I'm not fully asleep. I'm still conscious of my room all around me, but the edges of everything become fluid and soft, and the thoughts I'm thinking seem to turn into scenes in a play. All the figures are misty, like ghosts, and their words come to me from very far away. My dreams at night are quite different. When I'm fully asleep, I go into strange rooms, move in strange landscapes, and the people are like real people, but twisted somehow, contorted. In my dreams at night, everything looks as if it were being reflected in a fairground mirror.

FANTIN LATOUR. 1900. Large spreading shrub. Very palest pink.
These bushes are in a round bed at the front of the house. The flowers this year are so abundant that the tips of the branches are weighed down, sweeping the ground.

How melodramatic I've become, just lying here! It's this house. I wish I could be back at school, at Egerton Hall. I wouldn't want to speak there either, but I could lie on my bed in the Tower Room and Bella and Megan, my friends, would be there. I wonder what my parents have told them. That I am ill? That I must not be disturbed by letters or visits? I cannot even ask these questions. If I were in the Tower Room, Megan and Bella would chat away, and I could listen and everything would be plain. The food. The clothes. The decoration of the room. I like thinking about all the brown wooden desks in the classroom, lined up so straight in their rows that it makes you feel safe.

At first, when I was sent to Egerton Hall, I didn't feel safe at all. Everything there was so different from what I'd been used to. The building was terrifying: big and dark on the night I arrived, exactly as I imagined a prison to be. Then, inside, everything was so . . . I can't think of the right word. Empty? Clean? Unadorned? All three, perhaps. I can remember being taken down corridors where the walls were painted green up to the level of my shoulders, and then white up to the ceiling, and the green and white unrolled like two smooth ribbons with not one single picture to interrupt the flow. In my dormitory, the strip of carpet stretched on and on past ten identical cubicles on the right and another ten on the left. I cried in my bed to think of myself in these deserts, these vast, pale spaces, and I longed, longed, longed for the clutter of my home, and the houses, like those belonging to my aunts, that I had been used to.

I *do* have an awful lot of aunts. Bella and Megan could never get over it.

'Wherever do they all come from?' Bella said once. 'I mean, Alice, honestly, it's indecent. No one has thirteen aunts.' They aren't all real aunts, of course. Some are great-aunts, or aunts by marriage. There are aunts of all shapes and sizes and ages, although I can see that to Bella and Megan, who were not used to them, they must all have looked very old and doddery. Not one of them has a child, therefore all their maternal devotion is focused on me.

'But,' said Bella, 'they're frightfully aristocratic and romantic and exciting as well. Maybe that's because some of them are foreign.'

That was true. Long ago, my father's grandparents came from Russia and my mother's from France. My great-grandfather's real name was Gregorovitch, which he changed to Gregson.

'It's how they dress,' said Megan. 'They don't dress like aunts.'

'How do aunts dress?' I asked.

'Well,' said Megan, 'I don't know really. Suits, I suppose, in tweed or wool.'

'And felt hats,' Bella added. 'Usually beige or brown.'

'And dreary shoes.' Megan was laughing by now.

'Crepey stockings,' Bella giggled, 'and knitted gloves.' Anything less like my aunts it would be difficult to imagine. Most of them went in for lace collars and cameo brooches the size of belt buckles, amethyst chokers, chiffon scarves and high-buttoned boots. Daphne, one of the younger aunts, was tremendously smart, always dressed in the latest styles as laid down by Vogue.

'What about uncles?' Bella wanted to know. 'There seems to be a marked shortage of uncles.'

There were photographs of men wearing monocles and moustaches on various mantelpieces in my aunts' houses, but most of the uncles, it's true, had either died or been divorced. This didn't seem to worry my aunts at all. Some of them lived together in a big house in London, some had cottages scattered around the Home Counties, and then of course there was the detached Violette, who lived in Paris.

'What's the matter with her?' Bella asked.

I said: 'Well, she's a bit strange. Bohemian. According to Aunt Myrtle, she never washes and lives in a hovel with an impoverished painter and does nothing but complain about how well off the others are while she's starving, etc. And Aunt Daphne can't forgive her for wearing nothing but black. "One cannot help being ugly," Aunt Daphne says, "but one has a duty to be smart at all costs."'

'She sounds super,' Bella said. 'Let's get her to take us out one Sunday. She could come to Chapel and scare the living daylights out of the Juniors.'

'I've never even met her,' I said. 'I don't think she's been to England since my christening.'

Bella and Megan cheered me up on my first night at Egerton Hall and decided that I needed looking after. I suppose in a lot of ways I still do. I was hopeless at all the ordinary things when I first went to school, like getting all my dirty clothes into the laundry bag at the right moment on the right day. I always forgot, and then Bella or Megan would have to go chasing round to find me (in the long grass in front of Junior House, usually, at least during the summer term) and get me to do it. I wasn't very good at piling up plates and taking them to the serving hatch at the end of meals, or carrying huge silvery bowls full of watery stew from the serving hatch to the table.

'It's because she's a princess,' Bella would explain. She and Megan always teased me like that. They call this house 'The

Castle Next Door', but it isn't a castle really, only a rather large house, with a very big garden. Over the years, I've got used to the teasing, but it still annoys me sometimes. Once Bella gets an idea into her head, she'll go on and on about it, so I suppose I'm stuck with Princess. Bella's house is almost as big as this, even though it's got a much smaller garden because of being in a town.

My room runs the whole depth of the house. One large window faces south, and I can see almost the entire garden, right up to the gate at the foot of the drive. The window at the other end of the room faces north, and from it I have a good view of the terraces, the rose arbour, the kitchen garden and the beginnings of the orchard, which marks the furthest part of the property.

I can also see the summerhouse, but I don't look at it.

From a small round window near my bed, I can see the front of the house, looking like a yellowy-grey cliff with seven enormous windows set into it. The roses that climb along the walls are overgrown. No one has dead-headed them, and they have all become straggly, wilder. That's how they seem to me. It's as though my father has done no work in the garden since the night of the party. I can't speak of it though, and when they come to visit me, I lie like marble and can't bear to open my eyes to look at them.

The dormitories in the Junior House were called things like 'Rose', 'Violet', 'Blue' and 'Green', and the strip of carpet running down the centre of the room matched the name. So did the curtains that you could pull across the entrance to your cubie. That was what we called them. In each one, there was only room for a bed, a chest-of-drawers and a cupboard as narrow as a coffin standing up. There was a swing mirror on each dressing table. Everyone put pictures in leather frames on top of their chest-of-drawers. I had one of my father and mother taken in front of the house. There was also a photograph taken at my christening. I kept it because it included every single aunt, except for the dreaded Violette, of course. We used to pore over it, Megan and Bella and I, comparing hats and dresses, giving each aunt a mark out of ten for beauty, or sex appeal, which Bella insisted was something quite different. I was on my mother's lap in the photograph, wearing a christening dress which spilled over her knees in a white waterfall of lace.

I have slept in this room ever since my birth. I love this room. I don't care if I never leave it again. Because of the wide windows at either end, I feel as if the garden and the sky and the weather outside are drawn into it, are a part of it. It was newly decorated last year. I helped my mother to choose everything and it's almost as if I'd known I would be here for a long time. There is embroidery on the edges of my pillowcase. In one corner, there's my wardrobe, which is too dark for the room. Its doors are carved into strange and complicated patterns. Sometimes I think I can see something I recognize: an animal or a plant, but when I look again, it's gone and what remain are wonderful curves and lines and whorls chiselled out of the wood. When I was a little girl, I think I was frightened each night of what might be hidden in the black spaces behind the wardrobe door. My mother used to look inside it, to reassure me, but still, once she'd turned the light out and gone downstairs, I sometimes worried that it (whatever it was) had tricked her. Perhaps it was still there, rustling among my dresses, lying flat behind my shoes, preparing itself to pounce.

I'm not afraid of that any more. On the contrary, I wish occasionally that I could put myself on a coathanger and hide in there, flanked by my dresses, behind the carved, black wood of that comfortingly solid door.

OEILLET PARFAIT. 1841. Pink, carnation-like flowers.
The neat bushes above the terrace have lost their shape, and the roses are spilling over the rims of the stone urns in which they grow.

My Aunt Daphne came with me and my mother to a shop in London called Daniel Neal's to 'help' with choosing my school uniform.

'But there's no choosing to do, Daphne,' my mother insisted. 'I've got the school list. It's all down here in the minutest detail.'

Daphne sniffed. 'It won't do any harm. At least I shall see that the poor child's hideous things fit properly. It's amazing what a difference a well-fitting garment makes. Not so many people realize that . . . it's the great secret of true chic.'

Aunt Daphne's 'great secret of true chic' changed every day. Sometimes it was colour, sometimes cut, sometimes fit. On occasion, she'd branch out and then it would be black court shoes, or a certain perfume, or spotted veils on hats, or pure silk or cashmere. With the Egerton Hall uniform, though, fit was the only comfort she could find.

As the afternoon went by (formal blouses, games blouses, tunics, a cloak, a suit for Sundays, tie, hat, fawn socks) Aunt Daphne became more and more gloomy, but I thought it was wonderful. All these things were to be marked with my name and folded in my very own trunk with my name painted in shiny black letters on the lid. I knew about the trunk because we'd bought it already, and it was waiting at home. My father, I remembered, patted it rather nervously the first time he saw it, and said:

'My word, Alice, this is something, isn't it? All these brass clasps and wooden bands all over the place. One would think you were going to sea for a year, and not a couple of miles down the road till Easter.'

He was right, in a way. The first time I went to Egerton Hall, I did feel it was an adventure, and for the first few nights it was a little like being marooned on a rather crowded desert island. Me and my trunk full of named and neatly folded clothes were off by ourselves in the world outside Arcadia House.

Bella was impressed with my school cloak. Aunt Daphne had insisted on sewing in a silky lining.

'Crikey!' she said when she first saw it. 'This is grand, isn't it?'

'My Aunt Daphne says . . .' I paused, not wanting to insult Bella's cloak with my aunt's pronouncement.

'Go on, tell us.'

'She says unlined wool looks poverty-stricken and besides, it isn't nearly as warm . . .'

'I'm sure she's quite right,' said Bella. 'And it looks tons nicer. I shall get my wicked stepmother to line mine next hols.'

When Bella came back the following term, her cloak had been transformed. My lining was discreet navy blue that matched the wool, but Bella's was a purply-maroon – not at all a uniform colour.

'They can't say anything,' she said. 'There's nothing in the rules about colours of linings.'

No one ever did say anything, although some of the staff frowned slightly whenever they saw it.

BOTZARIS. Damask. Pale green leaves. White, fragrant flowers.
This grows in the bed outside the drawing-room.
Someone should have removed the dead heads, but
they haven't. There are only a few flowers left.

Last term, I told Megan something about Angus, about what had happened when I was thirteen. I couldn't help it. But I told her only a version of the truth. For one thing, I implied that he was much older than me, but there was only a year between us. I also said my father had dismissed him from his job when the truth was he didn't have a job of his own. He only followed his father around, helping from time to time. I told Megan that I hadn't thought of Angus for ages, but that wasn't true, even then. I often used to dream about him. He never actually *did* anything in these dreams. He just stood there, but it was the way he looked at me that I didn't like. It frightened me. It felt as though he were looking at me with a mixture of hunger and loathing: as though I were a thing he was going to eat, but which he knew would make him ill, once he'd eaten it. It's difficult to explain. Angus's dad used to be a gardener in Arcadia House. Not the head gardener, who was called Mr Harris, but one of the under-gardeners who helped my father tend the roses.

'Worse than babies,' my mother used to say when I was small. 'Your father's garden babies are more troublesome than you are.'

Is that why I feel for the roses, I wonder? Do I really think, did I ever really think, even when I was a child, that they were somehow related to me? All I know is, Angus's dad helped with the roses, and Angus came with him sometimes. I saw him picking the flowers when he wasn't supposed to, and I told my father. I was only about seven or eight. I ran along the gravel paths shouting:

'Daddy, Daddy, Angus is picking the roses! You're not supposed to pick the roses, are you? Are you, Daddy?'

My father and Angus's father would frown and go, 'Tsk! tsk!' and Angus would stare at me with his wet mouth hanging open (it always looked open, red and horrid) and his eyes flashing a message at me that only I could understand: 'You'll be sorry,' they said to me, clear as clear. 'You just wait and I'll see to it that you're sorry.'

Oh, I only told Megan part of the story.

At the beginning of the Lent Term Megan fell in love with Simon, the new laboratory assistant. There was scaffolding up around our part of the school then, and Simon used to climb up and meet Megan until Dorothy, Megan's guardian, found out and made the most terrible scene, and Megan was expelled from Egerton Hall. Simon lost his job. They went to live in a bed-sitting room in London. Bella and I stayed in the Tower Room and missed Megan. We wrote to her, of course, but she never said anything in her letters about coming back to school. It was such a shock to see her, and when I did, when I noticed that all her beautiful hair had been cut off, I burst into tears. I couldn't help it. It was frightfully embarrassing, because it happened on the platform at Victoria Station, in front of flocks of Juniors and their parents and Miss Runciman and Miss Biddulph, who were the teachers on school train duty. I had never been back to Egerton Hall on the train before, because this house is only a few miles away. Last holidays, though, I'd been visiting Aunt Daphne and Aunt May in London and so I arranged to meet Bella at Victoria. I wasn't expecting to see Megan and neither was Bella, and we didn't recognize her at first. Bella said:

'I say, do look at that frightfully pale girl with the short fair hair . . . doesn't she look like . . . oh, heavens, Alice, it is! It's Megan!'

She started rushing up the platform towards this stranger, shouting: 'Megan! Oh, Megan! You've come back!' at the top of her voice. Startled second-formers and third-formers cleared a path for her, pushing to one side their weepy, fur-coated mamas, and clutching their school hats to their heads.

I followed in her wake, crying because Megan looked so different, and so ordinary now. She could have been anyone. Behind me, the crowds of uniformed bodies went on with their pushing and shoving and no one paid attention to Megan and Bella and me.

'It's so glamorous, Megan,' Bella was squealing. 'It's really' (she looked into the air for just the right word, waving her hands about as though to summon one down from the iron-work above our heads) '*avant-garde*!'

'What do you think, Alice?' Megan smiled at me. 'And why are you crying? Not on account of the hair, I hope?'

'Oh, no,' I lied. 'Just, I'm surprised to see you. And . . . *pleased*. I thought . . .'

It was impossible to speak. Miss Runciman approached us from one side, Miss Biddulph from the other, like a pair of well-trained sheepdogs.

'Come along, gels, if you're coming,' they said, shoving us along with their hands, sweeping us up into the tide of bodies. It took us ages to find somewhere to sit. We stepped over lacrosse sticks and cases and teddy-bears fastened on to the sides of satchels, and came to rest eventually in a crowded compartment full of lumpy girls who must have been from other houses because I hardly recognized any of them. By the time the train started and everything had settled down a little, the subject of hair had been dropped. I was glad. I didn't want to upset Megan, but I hated the new short style. Megan's plait . . . it was as much a part of her as an arm or a leg, and I thought of its loss as though it were an amputation.

That evening, in the Tower Room, she told us why she had come back, and how chilly Dorothy had been towards her.

'She was pretty chilly to us while you were gone,' Bella said. 'I can't think why, can you? Almost as if she blamed us . . . anyway, you're back now, although I can't imagine why. Don't you and Simon love one another any more?'

'Yes, we do,' Megan said. 'At least, I do. I don't know about him. I,' – she blushed – 'I ran away while he was at work. I couldn't bear to face him. If he'd been there, I couldn't have done it.'

'Did you miss Dorothy?' I asked. 'Is that why you've come back?'

Megan laughed. 'I missed you two, that's all. And Miss van der Leyden. And a few other things. The place. And I want to do the exams. That's the main thing.'

'How can you actually want to do the exams?' I said. I could never understand the way Megan and Bella felt about exams. Bella treated them as a kind of performance. She was going to be the star and that was that. A sort of glittery excitement filled her while she was doing them, a sparkle of achievement. Megan worked steadily and thoroughly, and when exams came she was calm and placid and well-organized. I used to feel cold and sick at the thought of them. Sometimes, worrying about them even stopped me from sleeping and there's very little that can do that.

'If I don't do them,' Megan said. 'I will have wasted all that work. And I want to go to University, to try for Oxford and Cambridge. I want to leave Egerton Hall. I need a new home, a new life.'

'But you and Simon had a home,' Bella cried. 'A love nest, high above the city.'

Megan giggled. 'You should have seen it! Honestly, Bella, a dingy bedsit is not a love nest, I promise you.'

'Well, I think it's jolly mean of you to leave Simon. His heart will be broken and he'll run away to sea or join the circus and you'll never see him again. Years from now, when you're an old, old lady he'll return, looking like a wizened and ancient gnome and he'll find you and remind you of your young love. You will then spend the sunset of your days together.'

'What nonsense!' Megan was putting her school blouses

very matter-of-factly into her chest-of-drawers. 'I expect,' she said after a short silence, 'I expect we'll write to one another.'

After breakfast, every morning, Miss Herbert used to read out the names of girls who had letters. Silence would fall over the dining-room. All the noisy munching of toast would stop while the roll was called. Some people's parents had distinctive writing paper. I always recognized Marjorie's nearly royal-blue envelopes, but as Bella used to say: 'There's no fun in her letters, so what's the point of looking out for them especially?' I was waiting for letters from Jean-Luc, who lived in France. When I first started writing to him I used to peer at the pile from wherever I was sitting to see if I could see a corner of French stamp sticking out. Things were better when he was sent to Senegal in Africa for his military service. His letters then came in air-mail envelopes that had red and blue flashes all round the edges. I could spot those sometimes even as Miss Herbert was walking to her place carrying the mail, but of course, such letters weren't always for me. There were an awful lot of girls whose parents lived overseas.

Sometimes I take Jean-Luc's letters out of my drawer and reread them. They comfort me. I scratch around in them looking for all the affectionate words.

'I wish,' he wrote in one of them, 'that you could be here in Africa with me. Imagine for yourself the sun. The sky all day is blue. There are real baboons near the camp. A family: *Monsieur, Madame, et tous les petits enfants . . . et ils parlent français*. Yes, monkeys who speak French! I speak to them each day. I tell them about you. They say: "*Oh, la belle Alice! Quelle chance que t'as!*" and I agree.'

CRISTATA. 1890. Clear pink flowers. Well-scented.
Prickly bush.

This rose grows on the orchard wall. The petals will have fallen to the ground and no one will have cleared them away.

This is the real story of what happened when I was thirteen, the story I didn't completely tell Megan. Sometimes I feel that if I'd said nothing, if I hadn't run to my father in floods of tears, Angus may have been so relieved that he would have left me alone out of gratitude instead of doing what he did. Instead of coming back. My father questioned me very closely and carefully at the time: what did he say? What did he do? How hard had he pulled at my skirt? Had I said anything to him? Had I *ever* said anything to him in the past that allowed him to assume that we were in some sense, friends? I remember the wrinkles of disgust in my father's face as he said this. He winced and recoiled as though the thought were too much to bear. I started crying again.

'We're not friends,' I sobbed. 'We're not! We're not! I hate him . . . he's always followed me round, ever since he came here. I hate him. Make him go away. Please. Please make him go away.'

And my father *did* make him go away, at least from the house and garden. I felt as though some dreadful wild beast had been locked up, after roaming the grounds for a long, long time. A wild beast with me as its prey. No, that's not quite right. There's something splendid, noble, admirable and graceful about the wildest of beasts. Angus was more like a reptile, a snake of some kind, sliding up behind me silently when I wasn't looking, hiding behind things as I passed, watching me with his bright, flat, dark eyes, waiting for his moment to strike. He was always there, just on the edge of my vision, wherever I walked in the garden. He had never spoken to me till that day, when he followed me into the greenhouse. I didn't know he was behind me.

'Miss Alice,' he said, and the s's hissed around my head. I looked over my shoulder and saw him standing close to me. I felt myself freezing up with terror, turning to stone.

'Miss Alice,' he said again and took a step towards me. 'You're so pretty.'

All I could think was: the door. I had to get to the door. I moved slightly to my right, thinking, if I can get past him, then I can run out, back up to the house. He put his hand on my arm to stop me. It was dry and rough, his hand, but I felt as though slime had touched me.

'Let go,' I managed to blurt out. 'I want to go. Leave my arm alone.'

'Aar, Miss Alice, just a little kiss now! That's all I ask.'

What I heard was hissing: Alisss . . . kisss . . . thass all . . . asssk. I thought: if he kisses me, I'll die. If he puts that horrible, wet mouth anywhere near me, anywhere on my skin, I shall die. I shook off his fingers, which were still on my arm, and lunged towards the greenhouse door.

'Aar, Miss Alice, don't go yet . . . please,' came the whining voice, the hissing. He moved to stop me, but I was gone. His hand closed on the fabric of my skirt, and he pulled, wanting to draw me towards him. I pulled as well, and instead of letting go, he clung on and the dress tore at the waistband. The noise of ripping was as loud as a pistol shot. Angus let go of my skirt at once. I ran up to the house, trembling. I've heard those words so often in my dreams . . . Miss Alice . . . please . . . kiss. Hissing and hissing in my ear, and his mouth drooling and slack, filling all my worst nightmares.

My nightmares were full of the scene for many months, but that was long ago. Now I dream more and more about what happened on the night of my party. At least, I think that's what my dreams are about. Last night, I was upstairs in her room with Miss van der Leyden, the Belgian under-matron at

Egerton Hall, but in dreams people can be who they are and someone else at the same time, and Miss van der Leyden looked like herself but acted and spoke like my aunt Daphne. I was supposed to be having my party dress fitted, but I was naked and Miss van der Leyden/Daphne didn't seem to realize this. She, they, fussed around my body as though it had a dress on, taking tucks in imaginary fabric and marking them with lines of silvery pins. It didn't hurt at all, having my skin pinned like that, but tiny drops of blood began appearing all over where I'd been pricked and Miss van der Leyden said in Aunt Daphne's voice:

'Oh, we can't have that! Blood is quite out this season. Take that blood off at once!'

That was when I woke up.

Megan must have been quite desperate to have had her hair cut like that. She's always been fussy about her plait. Most of us like to fiddle about with our hair, try different things with it, but Megan can't stand it. Two years ago, during World Refugee Year we were all trying to think of original ways of raising money. I made cards, with drawings of cats, and dogs and horses on them and people bought them to send for birthdays and things. Bella spent ages making toffee so hard that all our teeth felt as if they were coming out by the roots when we chewed it. But a girl called Katie in Brontë had the best idea of all. She started her own hairdressing salon. At first, people were nervous of going, but then it became clear that Katie was a dab hand with the rollers and the setting lotion, and everyone in Brontë was walking round with beautiful bouffant hairstyles.

'We're going,' said Bella. 'Did you see Jenny Martin's hair in Geography? It hid half the map of Scandinavia we had to copy from the board, it was so high! I can't wait.'

Megan didn't really want to go, but Bella can be such a nag.

'It's for a good cause, Megan,' she said, and Megan, haunted by a vision of thin children dragging heavy suitcases on to crowded trains, gave in, of course. Bella and I came away from Katie's salon looking tremendously glamorous, but Megan's hair was so long that all Katie could do with it was put it up in a French pleat and backcomb the front into the new shape called a beehive. We all told her she looked lovely, but she didn't, really. She looked quite wrong, like someone in fancy dress of some kind, and straight after Prep. she disappeared into the bathroom for ages and ages. When she came out again her plait was restored and she was back to normal.

MARIE LOUISE. 1913. Spreading bush. Large flat pink flowers. Strong, sweet scent.
This bush covers an enormous area now and all the flowers are crushed against the grass.

Arcadia House: it's the name embossed on every sheet of the notepaper my mother has sent from Harrods in London. Egerton Manor was what it was called in the old days, but my father renamed the house when he inherited it from his father. Arcadia, he told me, was an ancient classical paradise, and that was what he intended to turn the house and all its gardens into: a kind of Eden of his own, filled with roses.

There is a wall built round the garden and my father has trained climbing roses along every inch of its length so that now it is almost impossible to see the brickwork.

Since the day of the party, the air has been heavy and the afternoons thick with warmth. It is the time of the very longest days, when the yellow light lasts and lasts and turns mauve towards nine o'clock. Also, since the party, everything seems so quiet. Perhaps that's for me. Perhaps the doctor has said to them: Alice is sick and needs quiet. She needs the healing power of sleep. The whole house is hushed on my account. The stones in the wall are filled with sunlight. I can hear bees through the glass in my window, and their humming makes my eyelids heavy and I lie for hours on my bed, drowsing, while bars of sunlight find their way across my bed, striping my body with the heat. Then, suddenly, I remember and start up out of my sleep and feel cold and ill, and try to push the memory of those horrible hours out of my mind. I think of other things. I think about school, or Miss van der Leyden, or my parents.

My mother has stopped playing the piano. All my life, I have lived in a shower of notes: waterfalls of music cascading into the spaces of the house as long as I can remember. My mother loves – loved? – what Bella calls 'the watery composers': Schubert, Debussy, Chopin.

'But only nocturnes and waltzes,' Bella noticed at once. 'Never the marches and mazurkas.'

'She plays Bach,' I said in her defence.

'That's lucky,' Bella retorted. 'You'd all be entirely drowned otherwise.'

Now there's nothing. A dense, almost tangible silence seems to have fallen over the house. Or perhaps it's only in my head. Little children cover their eyes up and then they think they're quite invisible. Perhaps, because I have become silent, I think there is a universal silence all around me. Maybe.

Art is my favourite subject. I am good at it. I can draw things so that you can recognize them. That's not what good art is, according to Miss Picard. Good art, she says, is when you can see the thingness of a thing. It sounds like something from 'Alice in Wonderland' to me, but Miss Picard insists.

'The essential quality of a person or an object or a landscape – that's what we're after. The very soul of objects.' Miss Picard has dark hair and a pale face like the moon. She wears her hair in a bun and looks nothing like an art teacher. She teaches Still Life and Drawing. Miss Whittaker teaches Life Class and Lettering. She is tall, with wild, dark hair flying loose around her face. She concentrates not so much on the thingness of things as on harmony, order, symmetry, pattern. She points out the Art Nouveau tiles around the sink in the Studio, and follows the line of a lily with the tip of her finger, showing me how it curves and twists away again into a spiral of decoration unrelated to the object except by the needs of the pattern. She speaks of colour: obvious colour, subtle colour, muted colour, noisy colour. Colour is a star actor, she says, in the drama of life. Her word is: 'Look.' Look at everything, she tells me. Look at the underneath of things, and the backgrounds and the way objects sit together in a space. Look for asymmetry and sharp contrasts. Look at everything that's amazing, wonderful, not like life. She shows me pictures of teacups made out of fur, and watches melted and hung over bare branches in a kind of desert. I don't like some of the things she shows me.

I could draw in this book, but I'm not going to. If I drew this room and the objects in it, I would be bored very quickly. If I drew what I could see out of the window, I'd feel sad, because I want to walk about outside, and yet when I think of doing it, fears grip me and I feel sick. If I drew my thoughts, my fantasies, the things I think about when I'm not writing this, they would be ugly. People are impossible as well. My mother and father have become sad and quiet, and I don't want to draw them like that. I would draw Jean-Luc, but I've forgotten what he looked like. The whole of the inside of my head is taken up with another face, which leers and grunts at me when I'm not on my guard. It's a face like a twisted mask, and it fills me with dread and loathing. I can't draw, can't draw, mustn't draw.

*

For the Advanced Level exam, for my Free Choice, I chose to do a kind of portrait of Arcadia House: the front façade of the house at the bottom of the picture and stretching out behind it a kind of three-dimensional map of all the gardens, the summer house, the orchard and so on. I put a border round it and in the border I drew and coloured as many roses as I could remember. Miss Picard showed me all kinds of botanical volumes, so that the flowers would be correct. Miss Whittaker spoke to me about scale and perspective and ornament. We looked at every imaginable border from all over the world. I had a dream about my picture of Arcadia House last night. In my dream, Miss Whittaker and Miss Picard had asked to see me. They wanted me to change the picture.

'I don't think, dear,' said Miss Picard, 'that this is at all what the examiners will be looking for. Do consult your reference books more carefully.' She opened the same volumes I'd been studying and all the roses in it were black and withered, with unnaturally large thorns.

'And,' Miss Whittaker added, 'you've left out the maze.' I said: 'We haven't got a maze at Arcadia House.'

'Nonsense, child,' she laughed and her lips stretched wider and wider till her face seemed split in two. 'Everybody's got a maze.'

I wondered for a moment when I woke up whether my dream had really happened, but I'm almost sure that my real picture was sent off with all the others to the examiners.

LA FOLLETTE. 1910. Tea climber. Needs warmth and sun.
This year the stems have spread sideways, so that a fan shape of tangled wood hides nearly all the brickwork of the kitchen garden wall.

My mother and father, according to family legend, were perfectly happy before I was born. I was told this by my aunt Myrtle. She is the teller of stories, the one who knows the secrets, the feelings, the jealousies and loves and all the entanglements of relationships going back generations. A holiday with her is an education. She lives in a small cottage in the country and her lounge is a delightful clutter of papers, small bones from this or that animal skeleton and forgotten cups of tea sitting in chipped saucers that don't match. She smokes incessantly, putting her cigarettes out in the saucers, or throwing the stubs in the grate, where they smoulder briefly.

'Can't be bothered with a real fire,' she says. 'Not now that one can simply turn on a switch and Bob's your uncle! In my young days, the poor maids would have to get up before dawn and lay the dratted things. I always thought it was frightfully unfair, even as a child.' She snorted loudly. 'Is it any wonder Daisy calls me a dangerous Bolshevik?'

'Do go on about Mummy and Daddy,' I would say, guiding her back to the subject. Like many story tellers, she enjoyed the digressions, the asides, all the little bits and pieces outside the main narrative, the things (she would say) that spiced it up and made it interesting. That was all very well, and I enjoyed it too, but I did also want some information.

'Tell me,' I used to instruct her, 'about before I was born.'

'Your mother and father,' said Aunt Myrtle 'were as happy as two small kittens in a basket.'

I laughed. My mother, white-haired, shy, with her long, blue dresses and her long, pale hands, and my father, red-faced, thick-set, jolly . . . kittens in a basket.

'Your mother,' Aunt Myrtle went on 'was very beautiful. You are very like her, in fact. Your red hair and that fair, yet unfreckled skin – that's just what she was like. Of course, when your father met her and fell in love, there were voices raised against the match. Your mother was . . . well, let us simply say not too well-connected.'

'Poor, do you mean?'

'Yes, and with all those strange relatives. Well now, we're all used to Hortense and Ivy and Fleur but in those days . . . well, connections with those sorts of people – Bohemians, musicians, painters, writers and the like – were considered . . . shall we say a little daring. But nothing would stop your father, and besides, your mother and he were both of age. So in spite of all objections, they were married. It was actually during the ceremony that I heard Lily whisper: "I believe she has posed in the nude. That's what Daisy says, and she should know . . . at that Art school of hers . . . well, you can imagine the sorts of things that go on in such places!" and she shuddered with horror.' Aunt Myrtle looked steadily at me. 'I've never had any time for that sort of nonsense. Why shouldn't people with passable bodies display them for the purpose of encouraging artists? How is one to learn about Art except from Nature? You do Life Studies in your classes, don't you, Alice? You agree with me, I trust?'

I sighed. 'Of course I do, Aunt Myrtle, only do go on about the kittens in a basket.'

'Your father took her to Arcadia House. It was all quite different in those days. The first few months they were there, your father and an army of gardeners worked on the outside, cutting, pruning, uprooting, replanting and landscaping, and your mother and an army of painters and decorators, plasterers and glaziers worked on the inside, knocking holes through walls to make rooms larger, choosing fabrics, laying parquet, hanging lamps and mirrors everywhere, installing sinks and baths and basins and stoves and beautiful, beautiful central heating, which was by no means as commonplace then as it is today. There were those (naming no names, you understand) who muttered things about central heating turning you soft, and eroding your moral fibre, and yet the truth of the matter was that your parents made Arcadia House so comfortable that all of us went back there again and again and stayed for ages when we *did* go. There were times, my dear, when the house was so full of all of us, chattering and carrying on, that it resembled an hotel . . . perhaps one of those discreetly luxurious and tasteful "pensions" often found near Swiss lakes. They, too, I believe, are full of women with not enough to do and too much to talk about.

'So the years went on. The roses that your father planted grew and flourished and became quite well-known. One of the earliest articles about him and the garden with photographs appeared, I remember, just before the War.

'We were all beginning to be a little concerned that your mother (who by this time was not as young as she was) had not become pregnant . . . She and your father had been married for fourteen years . . . surely it was time.' Aunt Myrtle lit another cigarette and paced about the room. Then she looked at me.

'Your mother herself told me what happened then,' she said. 'I don't know whether anyone else knows the full story. I don't know if I should . . .'

'I shan't tell anyone, Aunt Myrtle. Do tell me. Please.'

'Very well.' She sighed and blew from between her lips a plume of smoke which curled up and up into the still air of the cottage and disappeared.

'This is what your mother told me while she was pregnant with you, remember. I haven't, as you know, had children of my own, but I do believe that all kinds of hormonal changes occur which make people a little bit . . . well, unreliable.'

'Do you mean,' I said, 'that my mother was lying to you? When she told you this story, whatever it was.'

'Oh, no, Alice. Never lying. No, all I'm saying is that in such a condition one's imagination is bound to be, well, altered, extended. What I'm saying is, your mother's fancy had probably been at work by the time she came to tell me about it.

'One afternoon late in September 1943,' Aunt Myrtle began, 'your mother took a train to London to meet your father. He was to have a 24 hour leave before being posted abroad. 6 p.m. to 6 p.m. He had been away, training and so forth, for some months. Your parents had arranged to have a quiet dinner together and spend the night in an hotel. I can understand that. They wanted to be alone during the very short time they had. It's difficult to convey to someone of your generation, Alice dear, how we felt in those days when there was the very real possibility that our loved ones might go to war and never come back.'

'It must have been dreadful,' I said. 'I *can* imagine how it felt. Exactly.'

'Can you, dear? Yes, perhaps you can. You do have, after all, the gift of imagination from me. Now, where was I? Ah, yes, your mother on the train . . . She told me that when she got on, all the carriages were crowded. There were soldiers leaning out of the windows and waving, she said, as the train left the station. She told me she had to step over people as she made her way down the corridor, looking into each compartment to see if there was a space for her anywhere at all. After what seemed to her miles of train, scores of rattling carriages, she found a compartment that had, miraculously, only one person in it. Emily went in at once and sat down on the opposite side of the compartment from the only other occupant: a woman. Your mother assumed this person was a widow, because she was wearing sober, greyish clothes, and a hat with a veil. A blue veil, thick as mist. I think your mother must have started the conversation – perhaps asked for a window to be opened – and before long the two ladies were talking like old friends. Emily told me – but *do* remember the hormones! – that it seemed to her as though the rest of the train had vanished away and that outside the closed door of the compartment there was nothing but the purple evening, rushing by. Because the lady's face was hidden (so your mother said) it was easy to talk to her, to confide in her, and what Emily confessed was her longing for a child, and the lengths to which she and your father had already gone in order to find out why they had not succeeded in conceiving one. Of course, they hadn't told anyone in the family about the doctors, the consultations, the specialists, the medical examinations. Can you imagine Rose and May sniffing around, waiting for results? They had gone through everything entirely on their own. All this and all her anguish your mother told the stranger. She wept and raged and apologized for her tears. The woman in the veiled hat said nothing. Then she stood up.

'"By this time tomorrow, there will be no more need to cry," she said, and then she left. Your mother thought that perhaps she was getting off the train at the next station, but she looked all along the platform and saw no sign of her at all. The compartment filled up almost at once with still more men in uniform, laden with kit bags, all very jolly on their way to London for some leave. Your mother forgot this woman whose face she'd never seen. She met your father that night and you were born exactly nine months later!'

'That woman predicted my conception!' I said. I loved the story. It didn't matter how many times I heard it, I still loved it. It made my birth, my whole existence, something special and wonderful.

'Well, dear,' said Aunt Myrtle, 'maybe she did and maybe she didn't. Maybe your mother was lulled by the motion of the train and dreamed it all. Maybe there was such a woman, and your mother misheard or misinterpreted what she said. Haven't you noticed how one quite often hears what one wants to hear and not what's said?'

'Nonsense, Aunt Myrtle. I was predicted and here I am! I refuse to believe all that stuff about beastly hormones and things.'

Aunt Myrtle laughed. 'It's certainly a better story the way Emily tells it. Let's leave it at that.'

Thinking about that now, writing about it, makes me feel sad for my poor mother. Would she have been so happy, I wonder, to discover she was pregnant, if she'd known that eighteen years later she would be tiptoeing round Arcadia House like a sleepwalker? Last night she told me that the piano had been covered in the dust sheets normally kept for those times when we're away from home. It won't wake up until my mother decides she wants to play again. That, I know, will depend on me. I have the power to bring Arcadia House back to life again, and I won't. Why should I, when this non-life, this dream-state, is so peaceful, so hushed? Oh, nothing, nothing can harm me here. I am safe, lying on my bed, on the apricot satin of my quilt. I am safe from everything.

Miss van der Leyden is still staying with us. She is better now, but she was ill for a long time. I was the only person in the whole school, I think, who ever went to visit her in hospital. Perhaps some of the staff went but I never saw them. I had to get special permission from Miss Herbert to go by myself. Bella was always too busy to come with me and in any case, she didn't really like Miss van der Leyden.

'All that needlework of hers bores me,' she'd say. 'It's not that I dislike the old girl, not really, but I've never been a special favourite like you, Alice.'

I went to see Miss van der Leyden because I remembered how kind she'd been to me when I first came to Egerton Hall. She'd taught me to knit and to crochet and she understood how much I missed my home.

'Like a little angel banished from Paradise,' she'd say, 'but concentrate on the yarn, *ma petite*, and watch the patterns grow. It does become possible after a while to console yourself with beauty, with things you have made.'

Miss van der Leyden's room was full of things she had made. She must have needed a lot of consolation.

I hated the hospital. I hated seeing her in that bed, her skin a kind of dirty yellow against the sheets. She looked shrunken. Her hands lying on the blankets looked like twisted roots of an old tree. The other old women in that long ward seemed crazy to me: toothless, drooling, snoring. One old lady was nearly bald. Another mumbled and picked at pieces of imaginary fluff. I came home and told my parents. I couldn't stop crying, every time I thought about it. I couldn't face the thought of visiting her again.

'We'll bring her here,' said my father. 'She can convalesce in Mrs Thanker's room.' Mrs Thanker had been the cook in Arcadia House long ago, and her room was right at the top of the house, under the cupola that crowned the opposite wing from the one where my room was. Mrs Thanker's room was practically an attic, but large and pleasantly-furnished with a good view of the garden.

It made me happy to have Miss van der Leyden here. She took to doing all the small sewing tasks around the house: mending curtains, sewing on buttons and seeing that clothes were in good repair. She also began making lace. She had a cushion and a lot of little wooden bobbins and silky white thread and lots and lots of tiny, golden pins, stuck into a felt pin-cushion I had made for her in the Lower Third. It was supposed to be a strawberry, but the green leaves I'd sewn on had long ago fallen off, and now it looked like a small, misshapen heart, pricked all over with little spears. I was learning to make lace. I don't know if I'll continue with it now, after what happened. I hope Miss van der Leyden is still making lace. My mother said, a few days ago, that she spends all her days unmoving in her chair, looking out of the window. Her hands are still. Her eyes are closed. She has done no mending or darning. Sometimes she comes down to look at me, but never stays. It hurts her to see me, my mother says, stretched out on the bed looking as though I were dead.

Bella and Megan teased me about Jean-Luc, right from the very first time I ever told them about meeting him. Megan wasn't quite so bad, but I could see that Bella thought the whole romance wasn't anything at all remarkable, just a boy writing to a girl. Lots of us, even in the junior forms, used to get the odd letter from time to time from a boy we'd met in the holidays. On Valentine's Day, the girls who'd received cards were gazed at by the rest of us with envy. If ever a real love letter did appear, it was passed around from hand to hand, and we'd all sit round in the S.C.R. or someone's study and look at it and ponder it, and debate the exact meaning of 'love from', or 'with love from' or 'very much love', and the precise weight on the emotional scale of 'Dearest' or 'Darling' or (best of all, we thought) 'My darling.' If Miss Doolittle, our English teacher, had heard us discussing all this she would have been thrilled, I'm quite sure. She was always trying to get us to see the difference that the placing of a word had in a line.

'"The rainbow comes and goes,"' she declaimed in one lesson. '"And lovely is the rose."' Then she looked at us intently and said:

'Can you see the resonance and accuracy of that "lovely"? Can you see how the whole weight of the line would be different if it were changed to, say, "The rose is lovely"?'

Bella's hand shot up.

'Yes, Bella?'

'You couldn't do that. What I mean is, Wordsworth wouldn't do that. The rhyme would be lost.'

'Quite right.' Miss Doolittle nodded and smiled enigmatically at all of us. 'The rhyme *would* be lost, and with it some of the magic, but if you were to change the word . . . say . . . "pretty is the rose" or "beauteous is the rose" that wouldn't have quite the same quality, would it?'

Bella wasn't going to give up her teasing of Miss Doolittle quite that easily.

'What if you were to say: "And lonely is the rose?" That sounds almost the same and the rhyme's still there. What's wrong with that?'

Miss Doolittle closed her eyes and sighed.

'That, Bella dear, would alter the *meaning*. Words, however evocative, do have to mean something, don't they? A lonely rose is quite different from a lovely one, don't you think? Lonely suggests that all the others are gone. Dead, perhaps. It gives a very autumnal feel to the line . . .' and so on and on they would go, while the rest of us lost interest and began looking out of the window or cleaning under our fingernails with the sharp edge of a page.

Jean-Luc's letters were in French sometimes and sometimes in English. Occasionally there was a mixture of languages. I only showed them to Bella and Megan. I never passed them round. Bella and Megan grew bored with them quite quickly. Megan was so taken up with Simon last term that she scarcely noticed what was going on, and Bella soon realized there weren't going to be what she called 'good bits' and got fed up with reading them. Bella liked 'good bits'. There were lots in *Lady Chatterley's Lover* but I didn't get far enough in the book to find any. I thought it was dreadfully dull. I did read *Peyton Place*, though, as Bella said there were masses of 'good bits' in that. It lay around the studies for ages with everybody reading those few pages so often that the book fell open at just the places everyone was looking for.

I never said anything to anybody, but I found the words

embarrassing. I could feel myself blushing when I read them and sometimes hot shivers would come over me at night when I thought about them. Sometimes I wished I didn't know Bella quite so well or like her quite so much. She was a real mine of information on matters sexual, and had no hesitation in handing out her knowledge whether you wanted it or not. Some of the things she told me, especially when we were very young, frightened me. I remember one frightening thing very well. It was in our first year in the Junior House. We were eleven, nearly twelve, and we were reading 'How Horatio Kept the Bridge' by Lord Macauley in English. We all liked it. 'Lars Porsena of Clusium by the nine gods he swore' swung along with a brave rhythm, and we enjoyed stories of courage. Then Miss Henry, our teacher, who was round-faced and fluffy-haired, happened to mention Shakespeare's poem 'The Rape of Lucrece'.

'What's a rape?' Bella wanted to know.

Miss Henry blushed and searched the four corners of the room for ages before she answered.

'It's . . . it's an attack, Bella. That's all. Now turn to page 89, please, all of you, and let us read "Mary, go and call the cattle home".'

Miss Henry avoided looking Bella straight in the face. Bella sensed immediately that Miss Henry was hiding something and so she began her researches, looking things up in dictionaries and thick books in the library. One night, after Lights Out, when she and I were sitting on Megan's bed, she told us the results of her enquiries.

'Rape,' she whispered, 'is not just an attack, like Miss Henry said. It's forcing someone to have sexual intercourse with you.'

'What's sexual intercourse?' Megan said. I was glad she had, because I wasn't quite sure either. Bella groaned.

'Don't you know anything? Don't you know how babies are made?'

'Of course we do,' said Megan.

'When it's in a book,' said Bella, 'it's called sexual intercourse.'

'But how,' I wanted to know, 'can you be forced . . .?' My mind, which hadn't really sorted out exactly what actually happened when babies were made, how everything fitted together, gave up completely. Bella, however, was never lost for an idea.

'Well,' she said, 'I expect the man hits the woman . . . frightens her . . .' Her voice faded to silence. 'I'm not altogether sure, actually.'

'Is that someone talking in there?' The dormitory prefect in her pink candlewick dressing-gown was standing in the doorway of the cubicle. 'Get back to your own beds at once or I'll send you to sit on the stairs.'

Sitting on the stairs was a horrible punishment. It was cold outside the dormitory and silent. The only thing that stopped you from being bored to death was fear: fear of the dark bit outside the bathroom, fear of something you couldn't put a name or a face to creeping up out of the darkness downstairs, and above all, fear of being found by a member of staff on her way to bed. No one ever sat on the stairs for more than twenty minutes or so, but it always seemed like half the night. I was only sent out there two or three times, and on those occasions, Megan and Bella both developed amazingly weak bladders and waved comfortingly at me on their way to the lavatory. How well they have both looked after me! How badly I'm now rewarding them!

I've never thought about it before, but perhaps that long-ago conversation with Megan and Bella is one of the things that has made me so fearful of men. Apart from my father, who is kind and loving, but a little remote from me, I've not known many boys or men in my life, only Jean-Luc. All my days seem to have been spent with women and girls. Men are different. Boys are different. Bigger, thicker, hairier, rougher, rather like large shaggy animals that might be quite nice when you get to know them, but are a little daunting at first. I used to think of the nice ones as big dogs, and the nasty ones I imagined as wolves. When I was a very small child, the story of Red Riding Hood gave me nightmares . . . the big, sharp teeth, and that tongue on her flesh, slimy and scraping at the same time, those furry arms round her, the breath like steam, the red eyes . . . I used to wake up screaming, and my mother would hug me and soothe me and say, over and over again:

'It's only a story, darling. Only a fairytale,' as if that made it any the less true or horrid.

At school, during the junior years, there was a Bath Rota. In the Junior house, each bathroom had three tubs in it and three washbasins, so there were always six girls in the room whenever it was time to have a bath. I used to dread it. I couldn't bear the idea that everyone was looking at me, at my body, and it amazed me that no one else seemed to mind all that much. They were quite matter of fact about it, even Megan. Bella actually liked it. Dressed only in a bathtowel, she would wiggle her hips and pretend to be a strip-tease dancer, or someone in a harem.

'And it's so interesting,' she'd say. 'Everyone's such a different shape from everybody else, and all their bits look different.' I'd burst out crying and say:

'I can't stand the thought of everyone discussing me or comparing me,' and Bella tried to cheer me up.

'They don't care a fig, Alice, honestly! They don't even notice. Half of them wouldn't notice anything that wasn't shaped like a pony. It's only me, truly. I'm just naturally curious, that's all. But I swear I shan't look at you.'

After a bit of swapping around, we managed to arrange it so that Megan, Bella and I all had our baths at the same time.

In Austen House, each bathroom has only one tub in it and a door that closes but does not lock. I always put the bathroom chair against the door so that no one could come in by accident.

I don't have baths any more. My mother gives me sponge baths in bed, as they do in a hospital. She lays a waterproof sheet down over my quilt and rolls me on to it. Then she takes off my nightdress and washes me and dries me. After that, she rolls me off the sheet and takes it away and folds it. Then she puts on a clean nightdress and brushes my hair. I lie there with my eyes closed and enjoy it. This is what it must feel like to be a tiny baby.

My mother leaves a chamber pot in my room, but I can't use it. The lavatory is next to my bedroom, and I wait until I know both my parents are somewhere else before I go there. I'm clever about it. I wait till they've just gone downstairs. I know they'd never come up again at once, so that's when I get off my bed and tiptoe out of my room. My parents know. I heard my mother say to my father across my bed in the early days:

'She must be leaving the room . . . sometimes. Isn't that a hopeful sign? It means she's conscious. Alive, not dead.'

My father, grey-faced, weary, answered:

'It means she doesn't want to speak to us, or see us, or anybody else. Isn't that a kind of death?' and he sighed.

It's funny how things you haven't thought about for ages just slide into your head when you lie on the quilt and let your thoughts drift. I remembered Prue Scott this morning. She left last year. After Junior House, she went into Eliot House and we hardly ever saw her. But I've just had a kind of vision of her as she used to be when we were juniors. I used to sit behind her in Scripture and she would spend the entire lesson constructing a tiny box out of paper stuck together with

Sellotape. She did it *so* carefully that all the ends were perfectly straight and the whole thing fitted together beautifully. Then she'd sharpen her pencil into the miniature box and when she'd finished, she'd close the little lid, screw the whole thing up in her fist, box and pencil shavings all mixed up together and throw the whole lot in what she and all of us then called 'the wacky B'. She did this over and over again through the Missionary Journeys of Saint Paul, through Other Faiths, for what seemed like weeks and weeks. Megan and Bella and I wondered if she could be mad.

'I mean,' I said, 'it's so pointless, isn't it? She spends ages and ages on it and then it's gone.'

'Mad,' Bella agreed. 'I don't mind that so much, but she's so ugly. All weedy and stringy with that mousey hair.'

Megan said: 'You can't dislike a person because of how they look. It's not fair. She might be really nice.'

'Ah, but she's not,' said Bella. 'So there. She's Harpic.'

'Whatever does that mean?' I asked. It was a new expression I'd never heard before. Bella in those days was forever saying things that I needed to have translated for me.

She giggled. 'Harpic is a toilet cleaner. It cleans round what they call the S-bend. Therefore, Prue Scott is . . . clean round the bend!'

I can remember how we laughed. Prue Scott went to secretarial college, I think. She's probably frightfully efficient and ordinary now and no longer makes those silly little boxes. If she could see me, she'd think I was the one who was Harpic.

THE BISHOP. 1821. Gallica. Upright bush. Clear cerise open flower fades to grey-purple at edges.
The lower panes of the French window in the drawing-room are now completely covered by this rose.

Miss van der Leyden came into my room a little while ago. She sat beside me on a chair near my bed and told me that she was going back to Egerton Hall. I heard her sniffing. With my eyes closed, I imagined her wiping away tears with a little hankie edged with lace. Soon, she would be back in her own room at school, getting ready for the beginning of term, arranging for the laundry to collect all those candlewick bedspreads, mending the torn cubicle curtains, cleaning the cupboards where the bandages and sticking plasters and bottles of Virol and cod liver oil live. She leaned over me before she left the room and kissed me on the forehead. I could smell her violet-scented toilet water and feel that her face was damp from crying.

'*Alice, ma petite fleur,*' she whispered, '*j'espère que tu vas me pardonner.*'

What does she want to be forgiven for? Does she really think she is responsible for my silence, my lack of movement? She probably thinks that if she'd said something different, done something else on the night of the party, all this might have been avoided. But everything happened before I went to her room. I went there to hide. I went there for comfort, peace. I wanted to get as far away as possible from the ground, from the garden.

Now Miss van der Leyden asks me to forgive her. There's nothing to forgive. I'm sorry she's leaving. I'm sorry I've made her sad.

Jean-Luc is the only young man I have ever met whom I would describe as 'beautiful'. Bella used to hold up pictures of actors and ask my opinion of them, and the best I could find to say was: 'Quite nice.'

'Alice, I could strangle you! Why are you so fussy?' she would growl, and grind her teeth at me.

I met Jean-Luc at my Aunt Lily's house in Eccleston

Square. His mother was a French countess and she and Aunt Lily were at finishing school together in Switzerland, years and years ago. Jean-Luc stood up to be introduced to me. Aunt Lily, who imagines she's still a debutante or a Bright Young Thing or something, wears a silk bandage affair tied round her forehead and smokes pink and blue and green Sobranie cigarettes, which look good enough to eat and far too pretty to go up in smoke.

'Darlings,' she crooned, 'you two are positively destined to be frightfully good chums! After all, Monique and I go back to before the Ark. Alice, this is Jean-Luc and don't you think he's a perfect poppet? Jean-Luc, this is the divine Alice . . . now we two ancient crones are going to show you into the study while we sip our G and Ts and dissect old friends.'

Jean-Luc shook my hand and smiled at me and blushed. I blushed too, but not because of my embarrassing aunt. I was used to her. No, I blushed because Jean-Luc was beautiful: fair and tall, with eyes the exact colour of the sky at twilight, between blue and mauve, and as I stared at him, I could feel him looking at me, and thinking I was beautiful, too.

We sat in the study that used to belong to Lily's late husband, Colin, who was my father's brother. Now I keep trying to bring back that conversation, to think myself into it again, to recall it. I can't really remember it, though, however hard I try. Part of the trouble was that we were talking French, and I was so worried about trying to get everything right that I couldn't concentrate properly. I told him about Egerton Hall, about my life there, and what I was studying, but all the time my mouth was making the sounds, I was thinking about how much I wanted to put my hand out and touch that hair, and about what it would be like if he were just to lean forward only a little in his chair and put his lips on my skin. Thinking this, I could feel a blush spreading up from my neck to cover my face, and at the same time, my stomach seemed to melt and squirm and tighten in a way I'd never felt before. He told me about his school, and about the military service he would be starting on his return to France. Perhaps, he said, he would be posted overseas. Would I consider writing to him? I said yes, of course, I'd love to. He took a notebook out of the inside pocket of his jacket, and I wrote my name and address in it.

'I haven't got a notebook,' I said, 'but there must be some paper here somewhere.' I found some old writing paper in a drawer of Uncle Colin's desk. Jean-Luc came over and stood beside me to write. Then he turned to me. (I do remember this. I don't remember other words, but I do remember this.)

'*Alice, je veux vous embrasser . . .*' he said, and I can remember thinking: he's calling me '*vous*' as though he hardly knows me. I couldn't even bring out the right words, the ones I wanted to say, in English, much less in French, so I just nodded. Then he kissed me. I've never spoken to anyone about that kiss, not Megan, not Bella, not anyone in the whole world. I couldn't describe it. I just knew I felt as if I had blossomed, as if every part of me were opening like a new rose. I don't know how long we stood there, drinking one another in, but Aunt Lily and Monique came giggling and clinking their glasses and we heard them as they walked along the passage, and sprang apart. Later, when we said goodbye, he kissed my hand.

That was the only time I've ever seen him. He used to write to me often, but just lately, in the last few months, the letters have tailed off. I haven't heard for four weeks now. I think he must have forgotten me. Perhaps he met someone else. Kissed someone else. Perhaps that one kiss means nothing to him any more. If you eat lots of delicious sweets, why should you even try to remember a tasty one you had months ago? The reason I haven't forgotten is because I consider Jean-Luc's kiss to be the only loving kiss I've ever had from someone other than my family. I used to dream about it, dream about him. One of the reasons I sleep so much is that I can sometimes be there for a while, in that study, close to him. Just lately, though, the Red Riding Hood dreams have started to come back.

Angus was in a dream I had last night. We were in the dining-room at Egerton Hall and I was at the top of the table because I was a prefect. I had to serve out the shepherd's pie, but as I handed out each plate, the person who took it was Angus. In the end, there was just me and six separate Anguses: three on each side of the table. The shepherd's pie had turned into something else – lumps of earth for the meat and where the potato should have been, grass.

'You can't eat here with such dirty hands,' I said to all the Anguses. 'Your hands are filthy.'

They didn't take any notice, but went on digging in the brown earth and green grass with knife-and-fork-sized trowels.

As soon as Megan came back, everything returned to what it was like before she left. I felt as though an important part of me that was missing had been replaced. I hated it while she was away. Every night, her empty bed in the Tower Room made me feel sad. Bella and I used to play a game of 'At this very moment Megan is . . .' and we'd think of all sorts of splendid and silly and downright impossible things for her to be doing. For a while after she'd gone, at least until the end of last term, everyone was talking about nothing else, gossiping, pretending they'd known all along about Simon and Megan, and making things up that we knew weren't true because Megan had told us so. We kept denying all this, Bella and I, but the more we denied the worse it became until all sorts of horrible stories were flying round the school: Megan and

Simon had been seen, half-naked, coming out of Chapel, Megan and Simon had been spotted in the pavilion during a lacrosse match, kissing behind the stacked-up cricket equipment, Simon had been seen with this or that member of staff in Egerton Magna, he'd been seen with his arms round Dorothy through the window of the stationery cupboard . . . all these rumours and much worse ones, ones that I can't even write down, began to circulate. Then, over the holidays, people forgot. Megan came back and smiled and said nothing. Dorothy, who'd been very chilly and sarcastic towards me and Bella, warmed up a little, although not much. She would nod her head in our direction if she saw us in the corridor. Maybe, we thought, by the time exams are here, she'll manage a smile.

Whenever we weren't working, or lying in the grass near the cricket field worrying about work we weren't doing, we would discuss the Grand Ball. This was the name Bella had given to my party, and for ages we used endlessly to talk about what we'd be wearing.

'Marjorie's being jolly mean,' said Bella. 'My whole life seems to be a series of quarrels and disagreements with my wicked stepmother.' She sighed and went on:

'I want absolutely acres of black satin – a huge skirt so that I can trail down all your staircases, Alice, looking frightfully dramatic. Or else very, very little material: a plain black sheath from neck to hem, with a long slit up the side and no back at all.'

Megan giggled. 'You'll look like a witch, Bella.'

'Don't you start!' Bella said. 'Marjorie said that. She also said, (and I doubt if I can do justice to her acid tones, but I'll try) "It'll be the very opposite of mutton dressed as lamb, darling. Too, too ageing for words."' Bella made a face. 'So I've given in. Compromised. I hate doing it, but there you are. Marjorie's paying after all. It's quite nice, actually.'

'Describe it,' Megan said. 'Go on.'

'Well,' said Bella, 'it's red. A wonderful, flaming, scarlet satin. And it's strapless. You should just see my creamy shoulders!'

'And are there yards and yards of fabric in the skirt?' I asked.

'Not really. It's quite discreet. Not straight exactly, but more tulip-shaped.'

'What's going to happen to sweeping down staircases?' Megan said.

'I shall have to confine myself to gliding gracefully across the parquet, or strolling elegantly over the lawns.'

I said: 'You will be banned from the lawns by my father if you're in your winkle-pickers.'

'I thought lawns were supposed to be pricked sometimes.'

'One hundred pairs of stiletto heels wouldn't prick. They'd . . . they'd . . .' I couldn't think of the right word.

'Churn up?' Bella suggested.

'Spoil?' That was Megan. 'I suppose that's putting it a bit mildly.'

'What about destroy?' I said.

We all agreed that Bella would have to wear flat pumps or be banished from the lawns altogether.

'There are gravel paths,' I pointed out. 'You could stick to those.'

Bella sighed. 'Enough about my dress. What are we going to do about Megan?'

'What about me?'

'Well,' said Bella, 'you simply can't wear that same old pink party dress again. Not to the Grand Ball.'

'I don't see why not,' Megan replied mildly. 'It still fits.'

'Don't you *want* a new dress?'

'I hate choosing,' Megan said, looking embarrassed.

'We'll help you, Alice and I. We've got exquisite taste, haven't we, Alice?'

'I have,' I said. 'I don't know about you.'

Bella and Megan couldn't stop laughing. I hardly ever make jokes, and they're so surprised when I say anything even mildly funny that it takes them ages to recover. When they did, we decided that we would go to London and choose Megan's dress during the few days before the exams when we were sent home to rest. Then it was time to go in for Prep. No one had talked about my dress, and even if they had, I would have changed the subject. I wanted it to be a surprise.

'I am,' Jean-Luc says in one of his last letters, 'beginning to forget English. I am also forgetting real French. I am learning Army talk, which is not like anything. I am eating Army food which is (I do not know the word in English) *déguelasse*. I am marching up and down in the sun. I have learned how a rifle is cleaned. *Sensat, n'est-ce pas?* I wish I could see you. Even for only half an hour. Thank you for the photograph. You are beautiful, but small and too far away. I think of you every day.'

Oh, I think of you, Jean-Luc, not only every day, but sometimes for hours on end.

The Empire Day Picnic on May 24th each year was an Egerton Hall tradition.

'It's a ghastly tradition,' said Bella, 'and someone ought to put a stop to it. Imagine: busloads of girls being driven to some remote corner of the countryside, or worse still, the seaside, and then being forced to wrestle with triangular cheeses in silver paper.'

'The hard-boiled eggs are nice,' said Megan.

'I squashed mine last year,' I said. 'Do you remember? We were at Pevensey Beach and it was freezing cold. I spent the whole of the picnic bundled up in my cloak. Anyway, I banged my egg against a pebble and squashed the whole thing.'

'Why can't they give us something different?' Bella

moaned. 'Those awful bread rolls gummed together with butter . . .'

'Marge,' said Megan.

'Sorry, yes, of course. Whoever heard of butter at Egerton Hall? Those terrible silver-wrapped cheeses and a rubbery tomato . . .'

'. . . and a packet of crisps and a chocolate biscuit,' I said, laughing.

On the coach, we planned the food for our ideal picnic.

'Cold chicken.' (Megan.)

'Asparagus.' (Bella.)

'Strawberries and cream.' (Me.)

'Champagne.' (Bella.)

'Prawn cocktail.' (Megan.)

'Chocolate cake.' (Me.)

'And,' said Bella, 'we wouldn't be having it in what the staff consider a leafy woodland glade, either. There's far too much wildlife. I really don't see why I should share every mouthful with droves of wasps.'

'It isn't droves,' said Megan. 'Not for wasps. You can't say "droves."'

'Don't be pedantic,' said Bella. 'I shall say what I like. Crowds of wasps, gangs of wasps, cohorts of wasps, clouds of wasps, bunches of wasps . . . whatever does it matter? I can't bear them anyway. I'd have my picnic indoors.'

'Then,' I said, 'it wouldn't be a picnic at all.'

'That'd be the best thing about it,' said Bella. 'It would just be a meal. I hate picnics and I love meals.'

PARVIFOLIA. 1664. Dwarf centifolia. Low twiggy bush. Small red flowers.
This grows beside the porch, and looks stunted, even though I know it's bred to be tiny. Its stems look like a bird's nest, all matted together.

My dress, the dress I wore to the Grand Ball . . . what have they done with it? Could my mother have given it to Miss van der Leyden to be mended? I never want to see it again. No one has spoken of it. My mother thinks, perhaps, that it isn't in the least important what happens to the dress, but it is, it is, and if ever I hear that it's mended or that it's being returned to my wardrobe, I shall cut it up with scissors into very small bits, or burn it, or maybe cut it up first and burn the bits after that. One way or another I would like it erased. Obliterated, annihilated, gone. When I think of it, all I can see is the way the fabric tore apart, ripped right through the hearts of all the flowers in the lace, and stains from sweaty hands all over the bodice, turning the ivory silk to grey, spoiling it for ever.

My dress . . . there had been a committee of aunts discussing it for months on end. It began last Christmas holidays at a tea-party given by Great-Aunt Hortense. Hortense isn't even a real aunt, only the mother-in-law of my mother's Aunt Fleur, and she looks like nothing so much as an elderly eagle dressed in lavender serge. On this occasion, Aunt Daphne, Aunt May and Aunt Myrtle were there from my mother's side of the family, and Aunt Daisy and Aunt Lily from my father's side had dropped in as well. The conversation turned to my eighteenth birthday, first to the day itself and then to the dress. They were all talking and talking around me and over my head as though I weren't there at all. Great-Aunt Hortense started. She said:

'If I were Emily, I would be very careful indeed about what I arranged. After what happened last time, I think I would keep the whole affair very quiet indeed.'

Aunt Myrtle said:

'That would be to play right into Violette's hands. Nothing would give her greater pleasure than to think we were all still fearful after all these years . . . I mean, did any of you actually *believe* her drunken babblings at the time?'

'I did,' Aunt Lily said. 'I've always believed it. I mean, I believe in ill-wishing anyway, and especially in this case.'

'*Tais-toi,*' said Great-Aunt Hortense, quite forgetting I was studying Advanced Level French. '*Pas devant l'enfant.*'

I ate another almond biscuit. It's more than time, I thought, that I found out some details about this ill-wishing that people had been hinting at for as long as I could remember. I decided to corner Aunt Myrtle on our way home and get her to tell me everything. Aunt Daphne laughed: 'Well, Alice has her artistic gifts from me and her beauty from Lily and her kindness from you, Fleur. If we are believers in those sorts of gifts, I think we have at least to consider . . . how shall I put it? . . . the other side of the coin.' Aunt May, who always looks to me like a sweet-pea flower that's been buffeted by a strong wind, with pale, wispy hair and a wafty sort of taste in frocks, said:

'So do you think Emily and William should make as little fuss as possible about this birthday?'

'No, no,' Aunt Daphne said. 'On the contrary, they should make as loud a noise as they can, I say. Be damned to Violette. Can you imagine the satisfaction it'll give her if we all go about feeling cowed?'

The others nodded. Aunt Daphne went on:

'Which means, of course, that we must start thinking about The Dress. Emily, as you know, has always said we could take charge of it.'

All the other aunts nodded and sipped their tea.

'I'd always imagined,' Aunt May said, as she began at last to cut the cake, 'Alice in the very palest turquoise, with frills. A frilled skirt. Possibly in tiers.'

'Pink,' said Aunt Lily. 'That's the colour for a young girl.'

'But pink can be so sugary and vulgar,' said Aunt Daphne. 'One has to be so careful to avoid looking doll-like.'

'I wasn't thinking of a *vulgar* pink, Daphne,' said Aunt Lily. 'Do credit me with a little taste. I meant, naturally, the very palest of pinks. The merest blush, that's all.'

Aunt Daphne sniffed to show her low opinion of pinks in general and Aunt Lily's pinks in particular.

'What about,' said Aunt May, intervening to smooth things over, 'yellow? Buttercup yellow chiffon? Alice would look sweet, don't you agree?'

No one really bothered to answer. Great-Aunt Hortense looked down the slopes of her nose. 'I,' she said, 'have always been an admirer of shades of mauve.'

'You can all,' said Aunt Daphne, 'say what you like, but the decision has already been taken. I have been keeping the fabric safe since the day Alice was born.'

Everyone turned to look at her. In matters to do with dress and style, we all listened to Aunt Daphne.

'Tell us,' breathed Aunt May. 'Tell us about the dress.'

'I have,' said Aunt Daphne, 'several yards of the very finest Italian silk, the colour of old ivory. I have also acquired a quantity of handmade Belgian lace. I envisage a simple style: high-waisted, the skirt of silk overlaid with the lace, and the lace rising like a kind of mist to surround the bare shoulders.'

Silence fell. Slices of Christmas cake lay unnoticed on plates as all the Aunts imagined how I would look. I imagined it too, and felt happy at the thought of it all: my dress, my party, my friends, my father's roses woven into a garland for my hair.

Aunt Myrtle said: 'Don't you think we ought to ask Alice for her opinion, Daphne? It is, after all, her special day.'

'Nonsense,' Aunt Daphne said. 'Alice will have the good sense to agree with me, won't you, child?'

Everyone looked at me as though they'd only just realized I was there.

'Yes, Aunt Daphne,' I said. 'I do agree with you. I think the dress sounds beautiful.'

I was so busy daydreaming about how I would look in June in my ivory silk dress that I quite forgot to ask Aunt Myrtle about what the ill-wishing could possibly mean. A fog had come down while we'd been in Great-Aunt Hortense's house, and we had to pick our way home carefully among the dimmed lights and the looming dark shapes of houses and traffic.

I never worried very much about having to wear school uniform. To me it always meant an extra few minutes in bed in the morning, because I knew what I was going to put on before I started. At home, it used to take me ages to decide. Megan doesn't think very much about clothes and would probably have been quite satisfied to wear uniform all the time. Bella, though, used to fume and rage every single morning, flinging on her shirt and tunic, tying her tie as though she meant to throttle herself, and keeping up a running commentary on what she would be putting on if she had a chance. As it was, she managed to make the skirt of her Sunday suit as tight as it could be without crippling her, her nylons were the sheerest you could buy, and on those occasions, like Saturday Night Dancing, when we were allowed home clothes, Bella's were the most flamboyant of anyone's. She was the first person in the school to get a pair of stiletto heels, and she wore them until they were banned for making pock-marks in the parquet floor of the hall.

'I don't see the point of living,' said Bella, white with anger, 'if all I can wear is Cuban heels.'

Two weeks after the beginning of last term, Miss Herbert sent me to the San. for a rest. She said I must be tired, worrying too much about the examinations, overwrought. She had come upon me walking around in my dressing-gown in the middle of the night. What she didn't realize was that I quite often did this. I like places at night when no one is there. I feel as though I can think better, seeing how things look in the near-darkness or the half-light, how they're transformed. I was in Study Passage when Miss Herbert saw me. She'd heard footsteps earlier on, as I'd walked past her door. At first, she thought I was sleepwalking. I mumbled something about looking up a passage in one of my text books and she frowned.

'Come and have a warm drink, Alice,' she said and took me into her drawing room. It was strange to see her in a woolly dressing-gown, with her feet in sensible, dark blue plush slippers. We'd often tried, Megan and Bella and I, to imagine Miss Herbert in her nightclothes, but it was hard not to think of her as being propped up against the pillows, still dressed in her good tweed suits.

She gave me cocoa that night and asked me if I was worried about my work.

'A little,' I admitted, and she nodded and then said she was going to send me to the San. for a couple of days, to rest. I was quite pleased. I'd been there once or twice before when I was ill, and I'd enjoyed the small treats we were allowed, like not having to wake up with the bell, and being able to listen to 'Housewives' Choice' and 'Music while you work' on the wireless. Sister, who looked after you when you were there, was kind but brisk . . . oh, I would enjoy the rest, there was no doubt about that, but I didn't know if lying around all day with nothing to do would stop me worrying. I've always worried about my work. There's nothing I do, nothing I write or draw or work out without also thinking immediately afterwards: did I do that properly? Should it have been different? Could it have been better if . . . and so on. I've tried to explain this to Bella and Megan and to my teachers over and over again, but although they say they understand, they don't, not really.

'It's like,' I said once, 'being at a crossroads and choosing a way to go and then wondering, all the time you're walking down that road, whether you wouldn't have got where you wanted more quickly if you'd taken another path.'

Bella and Megan laughed. Bella takes whichever road seems the most exciting and forgets about any other possibilities. Megan examines each road in turn, then chooses. If she finds she's on the wrong path, she comes back to the beginning and starts again. I wish I could be like them.

MADAME PLANTIER. 1835. Alba. Climbs high if trained up trees. Flowers open rich cream, turning later to white.
There are two rowan trees at the edge of the front terrace. The trunks of the trees are twined with woody stems. Rowan trees are supposed to bring good luck, but these are suffocating in the embrace of Madame Plantier.

It's a long time since I've walked about at night. Maybe tonight I'll creep out of this room when everyone is fast asleep, and see what the rest of the house looks like. Maybe I'll even step into the garden for a while. No one will ever know. It's very warm. No one will hear me. I'll be very quiet. My mother takes sleeping pills now, that the doctor gives her. My father drinks rather more than he used to, so that he, too, will sleep soundly. I know these things because my mother has told me about them. She sits for hours beside my bed, talking, and she talks quite freely because part of her believes I can hear nothing. She knows I'm not dead, she probably knows I'm not asleep when my eyes are closed, but it's as if I were absent, somewhere else, even though my body is stretched out on the bed in front of her eyes. I know I am hurting her, but I can't speak, and I can't move. No.

*

Dr Benyon comes to see me every few days. He checks my pulse and temperature and asks my parents about my diet. Last time he came the word 'consultant' was mentioned, and I also think I heard them say 'psychiatrist.' It seems that Dr Benyon has decided there's nothing very much wrong with me physically. I don't think he knows quite what's to be done about me. I think he wants some reinforcements. I don't care. Let them all come and stare at me. I shall lie here and allow myself to be looked at.

My mother came into my room at lunchtime with Aunt Fleur. It's the first time that Aunt Fleur has been to visit since the party. They whispered beside the bed. It's funny. My mother, I know, would give anything if I were to open my eyes and get up and speak and return to normal, and yet, whenever she's by my bed with somebody else, they whisper so as not to disturb me, not to wake me up. My mother even whispers when she's here by herself. Aunt Fleur has a very loud whisper. This is what they said:

Aunt Fleur: 'The poor lamb! How pale she is! Oh, it's dreadful, too dreadful! Is she . . .?'

My mother: 'We don't know. We don't know what she can hear. We don't know what she's thinking.'

Aunt Fleur: 'She's fretting, poor soul, and who can blame her? Oh, it's scandalous! Can't the Police do something?'

My mother: 'It's not a police, matter, Fleur.'

Aunt Fleur: 'I think it is. I think young men who go about doing what he did deserve to be locked up.'

My mother: 'I don't want Alice dragged through the courts. I . . . I don't think he will trouble us again. We are lucky it was not very much worse. It could have been . . . he could have . . .' (My mother's voice faded to nothing, then became firmer. She was making an effort to lighten the conversation.) 'The dress is ruined, of course.'

Aunt Fleur (taking out a hankie and wiping away a tear): 'Oh, the dress! How beautiful Alice looked in it. Even Hortense said so. She said to me. She said: "I think I may have been mistaken about the mauve."'

They've left the room now. I don't want to think about what they've said. When I think about it, a cloud of black floods into my mind. It's like stirring water that has a thick layer of mud at the bottom. When this layer is disturbed, the mud spreads everywhere, clouds everything and stains it dark. By tomorrow my head will be clearer. All the mud will have subsided to its usual place, and become a thick, oozing, slimy sediment in the very deepest part of my mind, until someone says something, or I think something that stirs it all up again.

I will write about the Ill-wishing very soon.

I've had the very worst Red Riding Hood dream I can imagine. Even thinking about it makes me shiver and I can't bear to close my eyes because then bits of it swim about in my head.

We were in the Tower Room, Bella, Megan and I. We were getting ready for bed, taking off our clothes and folding them on our chairs. Then we got into our beds. Megan said:

'Alice, would you mind brushing my hair?' and I said no, I wouldn't mind and I got out of bed and went to sit next to Megan, near where her pillows were. She leaned right forward so that I could give her hair a thorough brushing.

'It's long again, Megan,' I said. 'I like it better long.'

'I grew it especially for you,' she said. Her voice was funny. I brushed and brushed, amazed at how stubbornly it was braided together, at how much effort it took to separate the strands. Then I said:

'There, I've finished now,' and stood up.

'Thanks masses,' Megan said and leaned into her pillows,

but it wasn't Megan at all. The face under the hair was Angus's face: the thick lips and long teeth, the eyebrows that nearly met above the dark eyes, the tongue lolling in the mouth so that you could see how wet and red it was . . . and all crowned with Megan's hair. I ran to Bella's bed, frozen with horror.

'Bella,' I said. 'Look at Megan! Look what's happened!'

'Don't worry,' said Bella and she put her white arm round my shoulders as I sat beside her. 'It's only Megan.'

Then I looked again, and it *was* Megan and I felt a most wonderful relief. It must have been my imagination. I turned to Bella with a smile, and then started screaming and screaming to wake myself up, because in that split second that I looked at her, I saw she wasn't Bella at all. The face so close to mine was Angus's face and the arm round my shoulder was brown and covered in dark hairs and there was earth, brown earth under long fingernails.

Last night, because I was frightened of my nightmare returning, I left my room and went for a slow and silent walk around Arcadia House. The air outside was beautiful: somewhere between mauve and blue. It was two in the morning. Soon, it would be light, I thought, but I've still got time. I tiptoed downstairs and walked the full length of the house. I went into every room. All the flower vases were empty. In the dining-room, the drawing-room, the library and the study dust-sheets covered the furniture, as though no one was living there any more. The Den, the smallest and shabbiest room in the house, seemed to contain my parents' whole life. My father's pipes, some old newspapers, my mother's embroidery frame . . . I picked it up. It seemed to me that nothing had been added to the work since I saw it last. I couldn't see any letters for me anywhere, not from Megan and Bella and not from Jean-Luc. I hadn't really been expecting any. It was clear he had forgotten about me, and yet I'd hoped that somehow, somehow, a message would have reached him, through Aunt Lily and his mother. Normally, the Aunts knowing something would have been a guarantee that everyone else would know it a few hours later, but this? I don't think I've behaved badly, but maybe it's a disgrace having a niece who refuses to talk or get out of bed . . . people will say I've lost my mind. The Aunts are evidently keeping it dark, and when they turn their minds to secrecy, they're very good at it – almost as good as they are at gossiping and spreading stories.

I peeped through the glass door of the conservatory, but I didn't go in. All the succulents and cacti, all the plants in pots arranged around the white wrought-iron chairs and tables, seemed to have black leaves. I never did like the conservatory. The air in there was always thick with warmth and moisture, almost like a greenhouse, and you could smell the soil: a heavy, rich, brown smell flew up out of the pots and smothered me whenever I went into the room. The more elderly of the Aunts used to sit there for hours at a time, sipping tea among the creepers, like exotic old parrots in a jungle. My mother was in charge of watering these plants. She used to rustle between the flowerpots with a long-spouted watering-can in her hand, attending to each one in turn. Now, in the darkness, I was glad that it was impossible to see whether she was neglecting them.

The kitchen had hardly any food in it at all. No leftovers, no cakes in the tin, no store-cupboard filled with goodies from one of my mother's excursions to Fortnum and Mason's. It was obvious that my parents had no intention of entertaining in the near future. I opened the back door then and went outside.

It was that that made me cry: walking through the garden. Before last night, I'd have said that my father would have to be dead before he allowed such neglect to fall upon his roses. I didn't know, and would never have guessed, that all the careful, loving work that had gone into rearing them for years and years could have been undone in this short time. The summer had been warm, that was true, but still. I never expected such growth, so many stems knotted together, and twisting into strange shapes, so much decay, such brown petals and withered leaves, such a profusion of thorns. The climbers along the walls of the house were high and thick, clusters of pink and white and yellow roses beat their dying heads against closed windows. Bushes that had once been neat and rounded had spread, sending out rogue shoots along the ground. Anything that grew in a tub or an urn had spilled over and trailed its stems on the gravel. So many petals had fallen . . . Not one single rose had been looked at or touched by my father since the night of my party.

I went back to bed and cried and cried. I didn't go anywhere near the summerhouse.

I never knew there were so many tears! I went to bed crying, and this morning I've been crying since I woke up, because I didn't want my dream to end, ever. I saw Jean-Luc. I was at school, in Chapel, and for some reason sitting up with the Choir, to the left of the organ. All the Aunts were in the Parents' Gallery, in the front row, and Jean-Luc was sitting right at the end with his mother. He looked at me and smiled, all through the hymns and the prayers and when no one was looking, he signalled to me that we would meet outside after Matins was over. The guests left the gallery at the end of the service, and the Choir followed them. I could see him walking ahead of me through the cloisters. I began to run, and then he turned and smiled and came towards me and took my hand. I felt as though I were flying, flying . . . and then I woke up. I can close my eyes and see his face, but it's getting further and further away.

I feel better today. I want to write about The Ill-wishing. Now that Aunt Myrtle has told me all the details, I realize that if I'd only thought for a while, I could have stitched the story together for myself. I saw that for almost my whole life I've known parts of the tale, that it had been growing in me in the same way that a piece of grit in an oyster turns slowly, slowly into a pearl. Now that I see the pearl complete, I understand many things. I know that such curses are as rare as pearls. I also see why I'm here now, why I *must* be here. Such wishes are not to be trifled with, oh no. We obey them, we submit to them, they direct the course of our lives. I only began to understand this after my birthday. At first, I regarded it as yet another rather eccentric family story, and all through last term before the exams, I told Bella and Megan about it like a kind of serial.

I remember very clearly how it started. We'd gone in to Egerton Parva for our Sunday afternoon outing. Prefects were allowed to go into the village four times a term. There was a café there called The Old Forge which had low, dark beams, and horse brasses on the walls, and which served the most delicious Welsh rarebit and chips, and toasted teacakes with overlapping moons of butter melting into them.

'I think,' said Bella, 'that this must be what Heaven is like.' The corners of her mouth and parts of her chin were glistening and yellow. She licked her fingers and started wiping her face with a paper napkin. 'I love butter,' she announced, as if that were news. We were always having to stay behind after the Staff had left at breakfast, so that Bella could make raids on their table, bearing off triangles of brown toast and real butter to put on them.

'It's so unjust,' she would say, 'giving us marge and the Staff butter. I mean, we're the ones who are paying the fees. I think we should sign a petition or something.'

'Come on, Bella,' Megan always said, not really taking any notice, 'buck up or you'll be late for Chapel.'

Now, at The Old Forge, Bella looked around and said:

'I wonder if it's safe to have a cigarette?'

'Bella!' I was shocked. 'If anyone catches you, you'll be in awful trouble.'

'Yes, but do I care?'

'Of course you care,' said Megan. 'And even if you don't, we do. Besides, we don't want puffs of smoke blown in our faces.'

Megan was beginning to sound more cheerful. Part of the reason we'd decided to go out that day was to cheer Megan up. She'd heard from Simon that he was taking a teaching job in America.

'I wouldn't mind that so much,' Megan had said that morning, trying to look as though she hadn't been crying, 'it's that he thinks . . . he really *does* think . . . that I don't love him. He says I would never have come back to school if I'd really loved him. Nothing I write and tell him will convince him.'

Bella said, 'He'll discover how much he really misses you. Maybe you could go to America? Go there to university, I mean.'

Megan was very quiet. Then she said, 'I'm not sure if he would want me to. He's . . . he's quite angry with me. That's the worst thing of all.'

'What will you do, Megan?' I asked. I knew a little of how she felt. I hadn't heard from Jean-Luc for a long time.

Megan said, 'I'll wait. I'll do my exams and get on with my life and I'll wait.'

'Yes, but for how long?' asked Bella. 'I don't think I could manage more than a couple of months. Other men'd be catching my eye all the time.'

'My eye,' said Megan, 'doesn't get caught quite as easily as yours. I shall wait forever.'

She said it briskly, practically, as if she were saying: I shall wait till Thursday. I could see she meant it.

'I vote,' said Bella, 'we forget all about Love and soppiness of every shape and form and go and guzzle Welsh rarebits at The Old Forge. There isn't a heartache in the world that doesn't feel better after a pile of golden chips and a couple of scrumptious tea-cakes.'

Bella was right. We did feel better. By the time tea was over, we could hardly move.

'Let's walk back to school,' said Megan, 'otherwise I'll fall asleep.'

'Oh, Lord, really?' Bella groaned. 'Walking's such a bore!'

'No, come on, Bella, it'll be good fun,' I said. Bella looked unconvinced. 'I'll tell you a story.'

'You never tell stories, Alice,' said Bella. 'You paint pictures. I don't know if your story's going to be worth missing the bus for.'

'It is,' I said to her. 'I don't know if I can tell it properly, but it's about an Ill-wishing.'

'You mean a curse?' Bella looked happier instantly.

'They call it The Ill-wishing in my family,' I said.

'It sounds blissful! I'm mad about things like that. Who's had this malediction put upon them?'

'Me.'

Bella looked so shocked that I giggled. At that moment, she would have followed me to Timbuctoo, just to hear the story.

'Well,' she said, when she'd recovered, 'you'd better tell us all about it.'

So we set off along the road to school and I started to tell them about the Christening.

FELICITÉ PARMENTIER. 1894. Flowers open palest buff-pink and turn white.

I can see this rose to the left of the steps leading down to the first terrace. This year the white pompoms of the flowers are turning brown and withering very early.

'It all started,' I said to Megan and Bella, 'when I was born. I think the Aunts had given up any hope of my mother ever producing a child, and so, when they discovered that she was pregnant, they all began preparing for the event as if my mother were some kind of queen. It was wartime, as well, don't forget. Festivities were harder to organize. I mean, there were food shortages and no one gave much thought to luxuries.

'I first heard about my birth during a tea-party at my Aunt May's house. Aunt May is dithery. She's shy and tall and nearly pretty, but she has a faded look about her, somehow. Since her divorce (which happened before I was born) she seems to have started having slightly too much sherry during the long afternoons. That's family gossip. She's not what my father would call "falling down drunk" but spends a great deal of time in a state that's, well, a bit squiffy.'

'Squiffy?' Bella snorted. 'I like that. "I'm feeling a bit squiffy." I shall use it.'

'They also say "squiffed" in my family,' I continued. 'But squiffy or not, Aunt May's rather dingy little flat was part of the tea-circuit. Aunts would gather there every couple of months or so and my mother would always take me. Later on I came to realize that one of the main reasons for the tea-parties was so that I could be inspected; so that all of them could kiss me and finger my hair and clothes and turn me round and make me recite nursery rhymes I'd learned at school, and play silly little tunes on the piano. They were seeing, said my mother, how I was coming along.

'Well, that day at Aunt May's, Great-Aunt Hortense began to talk about my birth out of the blue. Maybe it was getting near my birthday, I can't remember. But she said: "I'll never forget the night Alice was born. It had been such a fine day. Then at five o'clock the clouds began gathering on the horizon. Daphne, Marguerite and I were at Arcadia House, doing our best for the layette. And, my dears, you cannot imagine how difficult it was, preparing for a baby in those dark days! We had cut up silk peignoirs to make dresses and robes, we had undone suitable cardigans and jumpers to knit into small jackets, we had all begun smocking and embroidering and quilting the minute we'd heard about the pregnancy, but just before the birth we were at fever pitch. Daisy had insisted we use her wedding veil of handmade Belgian lace for a christening robe, but I can still remember how she shivered and turned pale the day that Daphne first cut into it with her scissors. So there we were, stitching and snipping and talking and wondering and outside the sky was turning purple and the clouds seemed to lie so low over the garden that we could have reached out and touched them. William was with us. He was convalescing, after having been wounded in action. Emily, I recall, couldn't settle to anything. First, she tried to read and couldn't get comfortable, then we tried to persuade her into a gentle game of whist, but her attention kept wandering.

'I'm going out,' she declared finally. 'I'm going for a walk.'

'But it's nearly dark, dear,' Daphne said.

'And I can hear thunder,' Marguerite added, and William said:

'Let me come with you, dear.'

'No,' said Emily. 'I want to be by myself. I shan't be long.'

'Take a shawl, dear,' I can remember saying, 'in case it's turned chilly with all those clouds.'

Emily picked up a shawl and left. It wasn't too long after that that the clouds let fall the weight of water they'd been holding. I've never seen rain like that before or since. Sheets of it swept against the drawing-room window, torrents of it flattened the roses and pulped the petals where they fell on the gravel paths and the grass. A wind came up to lash the rain into even greater frenzies and lightning sliced and zigzagged through the sky – and Emily was out in this storm. William ran out at once to look for her, and although it was perhaps a mere ten minutes till they returned, the time seemed to stretch out for ever. We fluttered against the window-panes like so many moths, but it was impossible to see anything. At last, they returned. William was carrying Emily in his arms. Her shawl dripped on to the hall carpet and no one cared. Her hair was soaked, hanging down over William's arm like rope. Her eyes were closed and she was as pale as death.

'It's started,' William whispered. 'The baby's coming.'

We had all been, I realized at that moment, waiting like actors in a play for the drama to begin. Now that it had begun, we all moved to take up our positions, speak the right lines, play our parts. Marguerite came into her own. She had been a midwife, years ago, and began to oversee the boiling of water, the preparation of the bed and the warming-up and drying of poor Emily."'

'Oh, Lord,' said Bella. 'We'll be at school in a minute. Do get a move on, Alice! Can't you even manage to get yourself born before we have to stop?'

'I'll try,' I said. 'Great-Aunt Hortense made it very clear that she was not one to watch an actual birth.

'"All that blood," she said. "A messy business at best, and far better left to those who know about such things. No, I stayed in the drawing-room with William (who really did pace up and down like someone in a play) and a few more of the cowardly among us. Outside, the storm had decided it was time for a climax and on the stroke of eleven o'clock . . . I remember the chime starting . . . lightning and thunder crashed together over the very roof of Arcadia House, so that the fabric of the building shook and the sound of the clock was drowned and the drawing-room was all of a sudden illuminated by the ghastly flare of the lightning. Then the thunder stopped, the last stroke of the clock fell into the silence and then we heard it, over the splashing of the wind and the rain: a baby crying. William ran from the room, just as Daphne ran into it, saying:

'It's a girl! And she's a beauty!'"

'At this point, Great-Aunt Hortense would turn to me and I would blush and not know where to look.'

'That's only the beginning, though,' said Bella. 'There's not been one sniff of an Ill-wishing, as you call it. You're a fraud, Alice.'

'I'm not,' I said. 'I'll go on with the story tonight.'

'You'd better,' said Megan. 'We're dying of curiosity.'

OLD BLUSH. 1752. Climber. Smells of sweet peas. Pale pink.
These roses grow around the trees near the kitchen garden and this year they're growing in such profusion that the poor trees seem to be choking.

Now, lying here trying to make sense of everything, I imagine the night of my birth, and apart from the rain and the storm, it seems familiar. I think I must have looked very much like my mother as I lay in my father's arms on the night of my party, after he'd found me in the summerhouse and brought me back. I cannot remember anything of how I felt then. Everything was black in my head and spinning and whirling and all the faces I could see were stretched and distorted. But when I think of my mother, brought in like that on the night of my birth, I can stand back and see her and the Aunts gathered round her, shocked into silence for once, and it reminds me of myself.

*

'But what I want to know,' Bella said on the evening of our walk home from The Old Forge, 'is *why* the dreaded Violette was so dreaded. It can't just have been for wearing black and living in Paris.'

'No, it wasn't,' I said. 'It goes back a long way . . . long before I was born. Before even my father was born. Violette is my grandfather's elder sister.'

'Yes, but what did she *do*?' Bella was sitting on her bed in the Tower Room, filing her nails.

'It wasn't so much what she did, exactly, although that did have something to do with it. It was more what she was.'

'Right,' said Bella, flinging her nailfile on to the chest of drawers and leaping into bed, pulling the cover up to her chin. 'I'm ready for my bedtime story now. Tell.'

So I told. I'm not sure I told it properly, or made Megan and Bella understand what it was about Violette that made her such a powerful force among the Aunts. It's hard to make other people understand how your own family works. You have to explain things that can't really be unravelled: old resentments, rivalries that go back to childhood, strange attachments and loyalties.

Violette is my father's aunt. When she was born, my great-grandfather was already a wealthy man. She was a difficult child and a peculiar one. She didn't speak at all until she was three years old, and then began to utter whole sentences, full of complicated words which her relations were sure she couldn't understand. When she was three, my grandfather was born and Violette hated him. Apparently (this is according to one or another of the Aunts) she used to try to murder him at least once a week when he was a baby.

'Quite natural!' everyone said. 'Her nose is out of joint. She's jealous of all the attention the baby's getting. It'll pass.'

And it did pass, or maybe Violette simply gave up in the

face of the battalions of maids and nannies and attendants of one sort or another who were ranged around the baby to protect him. When he was eight and Violette was eleven, he was sent away to school. Violette was furious. She had to make do with governesses who taught her how to paint in watercolours and read to her from the more ladylike pages of French, German and English literature. As a revenge she taught herself Latin, Greek, Mathematics, Philosophy, Chemistry and Physics.

'Subjects,' as Great-Aunt Hortense once said, 'which in those days were considered rather dangerous for young gels to excel in. A smattering of knowledge was one thing. No one could blame a young woman for that, but to make oneself as clever and well-educated as the men . . . well, that wasn't the done thing at all, it did lessen one's chances, do you see, of finding a husband.'

Still, Violette's education might have been overlooked if she herself had been different, but she was quite remote from the pretty, creamy-bosomed beauties of her generation. She was very tall and thin with a nose that dominated the rest of her face. She had a very white skin, and hooded eyelids over her eyes so dark that they were almost black. Her hair was brown, but she made it black, dyeing it to the colour and shine of patent leather. She wore it on top of her head in a complex arrangement of braids, like many snakes twined into a knot.

'And her clothes!' Aunt Daphne always raised her hands in horror as she described them. 'You can't begin to imagine! Huge, billowing purple, scarlet and black tent-like creations that just hung down and floated out behind her. You must remember, dear, she has no bust to speak of . . . and then those terrible flat, black shoes. Almost like a man's shoes . . . oh, she was the laughing stock of all London.'

'Except,' Aunt Myrtle once told me, 'that no one dared to

laugh. Anyone who *did* laugh, anyone who slighted her in any way, anyone she even suspected was saying things behind her back . . . well, let us just say that unpleasant things began to happen to them.'

'What sort of things?' I asked.

'Oh, one woman's hair fell out. One of her neighbours developed the most frightful skin complaint. Another woman she regarded as a rival fell over and twisted her ankle. Once, a house she was staying in caught fire just after she'd left . . . No one could explain that . . . there seemed to be no visible cause. All sorts of things happened and so Violette acquired a reputation.'

'As a kind of a witch, do you mean? A reputation for magic powers?'

'Well, people are amazingly silly, aren't they? They *will* look for supernatural reasons for things, as though intelligence, malice and a will of iron couldn't wreak enough havoc all on their own.'

When their father died and was found to have left his entire fortune to his son, my grandfather, Violette took up with the most unsuitable person she could find: a penniless painter of no fixed address and no family at all. They set up home in Paris, where he painted pictures no one seemed to want to buy, and she lay about in cafés, talking of revenge, muttering into her coffee and letting their studio turn into a hovel. Occasionally, one of the Aunts used to visit her and back would come reports of horrors: dishes left to pile up beside the sink until there wasn't a clean cup left to drink from . . . sheets that were grey with dirt . . . a roof that let the rain in . . . no inside lavatory. Oh, the Aunts would cluck and mutter and shake their heads. Violette, it seemed, had gone from bad to worse. But she had an obsession with the family and in particular with her brother's child, my father. No one knew how she kept up with events, not really.

'But she had her spies in London,' Aunt Myrtle used to say, 'who sent her things . . . the announcement of his engagement to your mother, the account of the wedding that was in the paper, the article about Arcadia House and the cutting from the *Times*, Alice, announcing your birth. That,' Aunt Myrtle paused as she looked at me, 'should never have been sent. No, indeed.'

I sometimes used to wonder how different things would have been in our family if my father had tried to include the dreaded Violette a little . . . sent her an invitation to his wedding, perhaps, involved her in the life of Arcadia House, tried somehow to make amends for her being so completely disinherited, even gone to see her in Paris. I said this once to Aunt Fleur when I was about twelve and I was helping her in the kitchen, cutting out leaves of pastry to decorate a pie.

'Try to appease Violette?' She laughed and wiped a hand white with flour over her apron. 'You might just as well try to make friends with a hurricane.'

BELLE DES JARDINS. 1845. White flowers. Palest
pink shadowings and markings. Spoils easily in the rain.
The rose flowers along the drive. Its flowers are scarred
with mildew this year.

The next day, I continued my story for Megan and Bella. We were walking round the grounds of Egerton Hall after lunch and before lessons started again for the afternoon.

'The night before my christening party,' I said, 'the Aunts had dinner with my parents and I was left upstairs in my basket with a new nursery maid to look after me. I just lay there in my beautiful, white basket, waiting. I was always, my mother says, good and quiet and peaceful and no trouble to anyone.'

'But you must have been told about it so many times,' said Megan, 'that you can tell us every word that was said at the dinner.'

'I know what they spoke about,' I said. 'They spoke about all the gifts they would have liked to give me, if they could give abstract sorts of things.'

'Like what?' asked Bella.

'Well, like beauty and wealth, and grace,' I said.

'I don't see,' said Bella, 'that you've done too badly in the gifts department.'

'No,' I said, 'I've been really lucky. Anyway, they took turns round the table, each one saying both what she would have liked to give me, and what she actually was giving me. Then my mother made a most extraordinary discovery. She realized that all the real presents symbolized the gift that each aunt wanted to pass on to me.'

'How do you mean?' Megan asked.

'Well, Aunt May wanted me to have intelligence, so she gave me a book . . . a beautiful, leather-bound edition of *A Child's Garden of Verses*. Aunt Daphne wanted me to be artistic and she gave me a painting. Aunt Ivy thought that common-sense was easily the most important quality a person should have and she gave me a set of building bricks. Then there was Aunt Daisy, who thought of grace, and she gave me a little statuette of a dancer. Aunt Lily, who wanted to give me beauty gave me a real pearl necklace.'

'What about Great-Aunt Hortense?' Bella asked. 'What did she think was a good gift?'

'Wealth,' I answered. 'She bought me some shares in something or another.'

Megan and Bella laughed. 'Just the thing,' said Bella, 'that every baby is absolutely longing for! What else did you get?'

'I had two dolls from Aunt Petunia, who wanted to give me friendship.'

'That,' said Megan, pointing at Bella, 'must mean us.' She laughed.

'Of course it does. Then Aunt Fleur gave me a kitten,

because she thought I should learn kindness. Aunt Marigold gave me a heart-shaped locket for love. Aunt Rose thought courage was a desirable quality in a person. She gave me a sweet little pair of shoes. I still know where they are.'

'Shoes!' Bella was scornful. 'I don't see how they can represent courage. What have shoes got to do with courage? Anyway, Alice, you're not a bit courageous, so that proves my point. The shoes were not a huge success as a present.'

'She could hardly have given a baby a set of duelling pistols,' said Megan, 'now could she? Anyway, shoes are for stepping bravely forward through life in. That's what I think she meant.'

Bella groaned. 'It's all that poetry you write, Megan. It makes you see anything you like as a symbol of something else. Just ask anyone if shoes equals courage to them and see what kind of answer you get.'

'That,' said Megan, 'is because most people lack imagination.'

I said: 'That was Myrtle's gift . . . imagination.'

'Don't tell me,' said Bella. 'Let me guess. Imagination was represented by a coal-scuttle!'

'No, of course not, stupid!' I said. 'She gave me a book to write in.'

'An exercise book?' Megan was horrified.

'Oh, no, it was beautiful. The leaves were edged with gold and the cover was soft, red suede. I wish I still had it. I wish it were still empty. I filled it up with drawings and now my mother keeps it with all my other baby things: the christening robe and the dolls . . .'

'. . . and the Magic Shoes of Courage,' said Bella. 'Come on, that's the bell. I can see we're not going to get any maledictions today.' She started running towards Egerton Hall.

'Hang on!' I called after her. 'I can't run as fast as you do.'

'Those Aunts,' she shouted back over her shoulder, 'forgot to endow you with speed.' She dashed ahead of Megan and her laughter was carried back to us on the wind.

BLUSH NOISETTE. 1817. Climber. Flowers in clusters, cream shadowed with pink. Smells sweetly of cloves.
This rose is growing on the wall under my window. Green tendrils snake up the grey stone, feeling their way towards my windowsill.

Last night I dreamed of a road and a car going along a road. I couldn't see anything at the side of the road, only an asphalt ribbon unwinding in front of the car, and no landscape anywhere. The car was big and square and black, almost like a taxi. I couldn't see who was driving it, but I knew it was a woman. I could see her hands on the steering wheel, her long, red nails. As the car drove along everything grew darker, and then I realized that it was travelling up the drive of this house. Then the car stopped and the driver got out, but the soft black folds of the clothes she was wearing blew up and covered her over, and spread and spread, blotting out everything I could see. When I woke up, my quilt had slid up over my face.

Bella is the least patient person I know, but Megan will wait and wait for something she wants for ages. Every day since she came back to school, I noticed her looking at Miss Herbert's pile of letters, trying to guess whether there was one there from Simon. I could see how she almost held her breath, because I did the same thing myself, waiting for letters from Jean-Luc which arrived less and less frequently. I knew that Megan was missing Simon, even though she never said a word. She used to stand by the window of the Tower Room for ages, looking down, but the scaffolding that was there in January had been taken away.

Bella is quite different. She always told us exactly what she was feeling and thinking whether we were interested in hearing it or not, and when she wanted something, she always had to have it 'immediately if not sooner' – that was her expression. She kept on and on at me, nagging me about the story, the story of the malediction, and it didn't matter that I had to do my French revision or go to the Studio for an extra hour of Life drawing. Bella couldn't wait. In the end she cornered me in my study, just as I was sitting down to do a French Unseen.

'Never mind that now,' she said, 'you can do that later. Megan and I are parched. Gasping to hear what comes next.'

'Can't it wait for tonight?' I said. 'I'll tell you tonight, honestly.'

'Now,' said Bella, closing all the books on my desk and settling herself down in the armchair. 'Tell.'

So I sighed deeply and told them. I think they were both a little disappointed although of course they were too polite to say so. They hoped for something much more dramatic perhaps, or maybe it's the way I told the story. I know that I think it's frightening, but maybe maledictions are less terrifying if they're not directed at you. Maybe it's easier to ignore them and say you don't believe in them if you aren't the person chosen for . . . whatever it is. I can write about it calmly now, because, in a way, it's over. No, that's not quite right. What was supposed to happen, happened, but for me it's still going on.

The weather was perfect for my christening: a warm August day full of sunlight. I know this because I've seen the photographs and they all show my mother in a hat with a wide, lacy brim, and shadows sharp and black in the glare, and all the Aunts shading their eyes as they look into the camera. Great-Aunt Hortense and Aunt Ivy have fans and

Aunt Daphne is wearing sunglasses. I'm there too, in my mother's arms, outside the church, with my christening robe reaching almost to her knees.

After the ceremony, there was a party at Arcadia House. No one took any pictures of the food, but I know that it was set out on the long, polished table in the dining-room on the very best crockery. Everyone came in their finery, and examined me and left presents and ate and drank and later walked about among the roses, admiring what was left to admire after my father had filled every vase in the house. By about five o'clock in the afternoon, all the guests had gone and only the family was left. They gathered round my cradle. Aunt Marigold said:

'I've never seen so many presents in my life. Aren't people kind? Our gifts will be quite eclipsed.'

'Nonsense,' said Great-Aunt Hortense. 'No one else can give her what we can give . . . and I propose we begin our little ceremony now.'

'Where's Marguerite, though?' asked Aunt Myrtle.

'She'll be here soon,' said Aunt Ivy. 'I think she's seeing to matters in the kitchen.'

'Let us start without her, then,' said Great-Aunt Hortense. 'She can be so tiresome . . . really, the whole thing will be quite spoiled.'

This is what I've been told: one by one they came up to my mother and gave her their gifts: the pearls, the painting, the book, all the other presents.

'I was so entranced,' my mother told me, 'that I never noticed. Well, you can imagine . . . it'd been an exhausting day. All those people and the heat and up so early in the morning and the food and drink on top of that. I can tell you, by the time the aunts began their little ceremony, I was reeling. I never saw the sky grow dark or the rain begin to tap and tap on the windowpanes, announcing the coming of a storm. Suddenly, though, we all became aware of a commotion somewhere in the house: shouting, doors slamming, footsteps running along the corridors towards us. Then the doors of the drawing-room were flung open and at that very moment the first bolt of lightning flared in the sky and seemed to outline in white and livid light the enormously tall figure that had burst into the room. She (oh, she was clearly a woman) had her arms outspread for an instant. She was wearing some kind of long, black, cloaklike garment and it seemed to us all that for a fraction of a second every fold and seam was fiery, charged with a kind of electricity.

'"I don't suppose for one moment," she said in a voice like razor blades covered in treacle, "that anyone was expecting me." Just as she finished speaking, there was a roll of thunder in the distance.'

I can see the silence and shock that followed Violette's entrance. I can imagine it. After a while, everyone returned to some kind of normality, some kind of social chit-chat: how are you? How is Paris? How long are you staying? Violette answered politely, said she was dying for a drink, took off her black cloak to reveal a black dress underneath. ('Ten years out of date,' said Aunt Daphne.) Then she turned to my mother and smiled.

'I believe, darlings,' she said, 'that you've all just had the most divine christening party. Is it true?'

'Yes,' my mother whispered. 'For my daughter, Alice.'

'Alice . . .' Violette rummaged in her pockets, produced a packet of French cigarettes and lit one. 'Alice,' she said again and blew a cloud of acrid smoke into the air. 'May I see her?'

'Oh, yes,' said my mother. 'Yes, of course.'

My cradle was on the other side of the room, in a corner. It had been put there so that I could sleep away from the voices of the chattering aunts arranged around the fireplace in sofas and armchairs. My mother says that walking across the carpet with Violette to where I was lying seemed to go on for ever and ever.

'How pretty!' Violette said, and turning to my mother:

'How naughty you are, Emily, not to invite me to the christening! And William . . . well, it's what I've come to expect, but still, I should have thought that an occasion like this . . . never mind.' And Violette turned and went back to sit among the Aunts.

'And have you all given little Alice the most marvellous presents?' she murmured, accepting a gin and tonic. No one answered. Violette laughed.

'The thing is, you're all too, too predictable. Too safe. I know precisely what gifts you've given. All the usual things I'm quite sure. My gift,' she smiled, 'is more original. Quite different, really. Don't you think Death an original gift?' The aunts shifted in their seats. My mother turned white. The thunder was getting nearer, crashing round the house, shaking the windows. My father said:

'Violette, I know we haven't seen one another for many years, but I must ask you . . .'

'Ask me what? To leave? Oh, I left long ago. Can you sense something, William? Trouble perhaps? Is that why you'd rather I weren't here, spoiling the fun? I'll go, don't worry, but not before I've given the baby, Alice, my little present.' She laughed. 'I wasn't really serious, William, only I *do* think that even a little scrap like this should have a . . . what shall we call it? . . . a *memento mori*. A tiny reminder that even the prettiest rosebud does wither in the end.'

She stood up and strode over to the cradle. My mother and father flew after her. Violette pinned a jet mourning-brooch to the edge of the shawl I was wrapped in.

'Oh, don't worry, darlings!' she said. 'Stabbing young babies is not my style . . . not my style at all. No, you shall have your Alice for a while yet, but I do think it's such a waste, growing old. Don't you? That's what I wish for Alice: never to grow old. Just one last, magnificent final fling and then out like a candle. At eighteen, perhaps? Yes, like a candle. Extinguished.' Violette began to laugh.

'Please,' said my father. 'Please, Violette, you've been drinking. You're not yourself. I can see that. I implore you.'

'Don't implore,' said Violette. 'I'm leaving. I only came to bring my little gift and I have.'

The Aunts began to wail and moan. Violette put her cloak on, paused at the door and looked at my parents.

'You should have thought,' she said quietly, 'to invite me to your christening. I have no children, any more than the rest of you. I might have taken Alice under my wing. Ah, well, it's too late now, I suppose.' She slammed the door behind her and as she did so, lightning and thunder met and clashed over the roof of Arcadia House. The storm was now directly overhead. My mother ran to my cradle, unpinned the brooch and flung it away from her as though it were alive and poisonous. It was at this point that Aunt Marguerite came back from the kitchen.

'I'm sorry to have been so long,' she said, 'only one of the little helpers from the village was so frightened of the thunder that I had to comfort her, silly goose. Whatever's the matter here?'

The Aunts told her. My mother, half-fainting with terror, told her. Then the discussion began. Long into the night the arguments raged. Violette was powerless . . . Violette could do anything she wanted . . . believe her . . . not believe her . . . Alice is doomed . . . Alice is no more doomed than the next person. Back and forth went the words, and the tears flowed. Then Marguerite spoke.

'Listen,' she said. 'I haven't given Alice my gift yet. I could wish for something that would cancel out what Violette has said. I could . . . soften it a little.'

'But what?' asked Aunt Lily. 'What can you possibly give that we haven't already thought of?'

Aunt Marguerite chuckled. 'You're all so fancy and high-falutin' that you've overlooked something.'

'I never overlook anything,' said Great-Aunt Hortense. 'I must have considered it and thought better of it.'

'It's the gift I was going to give Alice all along,' said Aunt Marguerite. 'I've brought a lot of babies into this world and I know what's important and what isn't. I shall give the gift of health. I was going to wish her a long life. I expect,' she looked around at the gaping mouths and wide-open eyes staring at her in amazement, 'that now, what with Violette's wish, there may be an accident or an illness, or something of that kind, but Alice will live to a ripe old age. That's my wish.'

'But were your mother and father comforted by that?' Bella wanted to know when I'd finished telling her and Megan the story. 'I don't know if I would have been. Violette seems to be a much more dramatic and forceful character than Marguerite. Surely her wish would have more power?'

'If you believe in the power of wishes at all,' I said. 'I don't know whether I do or not.'

'Well, you should,' said Bella, 'because everything everyone wished you when you were born seems to have come true.'

'Then so will Aunt Marguerite's,' I said. 'If I believe in one wish, I must believe in them all. I don't see why the dreaded Violette's should be stronger than anyone else's.'

Bella didn't answer. She didn't need to. I knew what she was thinking. Death is a bit of a trump card. It's hard to think of anything more final than that.

Aunt Marguerite's wish was stronger in the end, though, wasn't it, Bella? Megan? Here I am still, not quite fully alive, but not in the condition Violette predicted. A long way away from that.

BELLE AMOUR. Alba. Pale pink flowers. Distinct in its thorns. Scent has a hint of aniseed.
This rose is straggling over the gravel of the drive, which looks dreadful from my window. The pink petals are speckled with brown, as though they've been scorched.

The exams seem to have happened a very long time ago and almost in another place, a place I find I can barely remember now. They seem to be unimportant and when I think of them (which isn't often) I can't imagine how it was that they filled my life for so long. From before the time Megan went away, right up until my birthday, they were all I ever thought about when I wasn't daydreaming about Jean-Luc. I worried about them. I used to sit for hours, learning quotations, going over essays, trying to make sense of everything, trying to pack items of knowledge into my head. I felt I was folding clothes into a suitcase . . . there and there, I said to myself, that's learned, I know that, put that in the case and close the lid before it can fly out again. Depending on my mood, I either felt that my suitcase was pleasantly full of neat little packages of information, all ready to be unwrapped when the exams arrived, or else that something, someone had robbed me in the night and my whole suitcase was empty and echoing and I wouldn't be able to find one single thing to offer up on paper.

Before the exams started, we were sent home for a few days of compulsory rest. No one was supposed to take any work with them, but of course we did. We all became as ingenious as diamond-smugglers, hiding our notes where no one would think to look for them – in boxes of sanitary towels, for example. Some pieces of paper were really tiny and could be rolled up tight and put inside hair rollers. That was Bella's idea.

'Actually,' she said. 'I think they're right. I feel we *should* rest. Anything we don't know by now we'll probably never learn.'

These words terrified me. Oh, I thought, as we packed for the days at home, how I long for it to be over! How much I want the inside of my head to be clear again, swept clean. Now, of course, I feel differently. Now I would love to have the subjunctive of '*faire*' to worry about, and nothing would please me more than reciting lists of quotations as long as my arm. It would be restful to do that again, instead of what I'm doing now: I'm thinking over everything that's taken place in the last few weeks and while I'm doing that, I'm also waiting. I don't know what I'm waiting for, but something, something is coming towards me from somewhere, and I will know what it is when I see it, or when I feel it. Meanwhile, I spend hours and hours sleeping and dreaming, and when I'm not doing that, I'm watching the roses.

BLANCHEFLEUR. 1835. Bunches of palest pink
flowers. Thorny growth. Very sweetly scented.
A tall vase in the study was filled with this rose on the night of my party. There are so many thorns along the stems.

Megan came to spend the days before the exams with me at Arcadia House. We had arranged to meet Bella in London one day, and we were all going to choose an evening dress with Megan.

'It's not going to be easy,' said Bella, taking a huge bite out of her Wimpy and slurping down some chocolate milkshake that was so thick it could barely travel through the straw. 'I don't know what style you are, Megan.'

'Something plain,' Megan said.

'But not boring,' I added. 'I think Megan should wear a dark colour.'

'Not too dark,' said Megan anxiously. 'I mean, not black, or navy or anything. It *is* June after all and not a funeral or anything.'

'You'd look lovely in black,' said Bella. 'It'd be tremendously chic, with your colouring.'

'But half the Aunts will be in black,' I pointed out. 'We don't want Megan mistaken for an Aunt.'

We must have gone into at least twenty shops. Megan was beginning to look desperate. We had turned down sequins, beads, chiffon, pleats, gathers, strapless, off the shoulder, halter-necked dresses in every colour of the rainbow. In the end, though, we found the perfect one for Megan. Even she had to admit it made her look beautiful.

'Not like a Scandinavian milkmaid at all,' said Bella. 'More like a water-nymph.'

The dress was made of taffeta in a colour that was neither blue or green, but both together. When Megan moved, the colours merged and blended in the fabric. The skirt was full, the bodice tight, and Megan's shoulders rose from the square-cut neckline like (Bella decided) 'newly-carved alabaster.'

'You'll put us all to shame,' she declared. 'Oh, it does make me furious to think of Simon missing this! He is quite, quite crazy.'

At the mention of Simon, Megan drooped visibly, just as though all her energy had left her. She turned to me.

'Alice, unzip this, will you please?'

I unzipped her lovely dress and she stepped out of it.

'You *are* taking it, though, aren't you?' Bella asked, and when Megan nodded, she said, 'Well, give it to me with the money and I'll go and get it wrapped while you dress.'

As soon as she had gone, Megan sat down on the little stool in the corner of the changing-room and looked at me. Tears stood in her eyes.

'He isn't coming back, Alice. I know he isn't.'

'How do you know?'

'I had a letter. Two days ago. From America.'

'You said that was a boring letter from your American pen-friend. Why didn't you tell us? What did he say?'

Megan sniffed and wiped her eyes and started pulling her skirt on.

'It just said he's accepted a job in the States for the summer. It said that maybe if he liked it there, he'd try to stay for longer. It said . . . well, I think what it was trying to say was goodbye.'

I couldn't think how to answer. Megan sounded normal again, but I could see she was still upset.

'Are you going to tell Bella?' I asked.

'Oh yes,' said Megan. 'Only not now.'

Megan told Bella in the Golden Egg Restaurant in Leicester Square. For once, Bella didn't make a joke about it. It was only later, when she was seeing us off at Victoria that she patted the paper bag that held Megan's dress and said:

'It'll be all right after the party. In this dress, you'll be gathering the young men up in bunches of six, like daffodils!'

On the train, Megan looked out of the window, and then at me and said:

'Bella's right, isn't she? I mean that would be the practical thing to do. I should look for someone else.'

'I suppose I should too,' I answered. 'I haven't heard from Jean-Luc for weeks and weeks. He must have forgotten all about me.'

The train clattered and shook through the outer suburbs of London.

'The trouble is,' I went on, 'I don't want to look for anyone else. No one else would be quite the same.'

Megan nodded. 'Exactly. That's exactly how I feel.'

I wonder what this dream means? I am wrapped in many,

many layers of newspaper, but I can still breathe and see. Someone is pulling the newspaper apart with their bare hands. Soon I can feel that it's all gone, and then I see him. It's Jean-Luc. In the middle of the dream I think: it's Jean-Luc. Why am I not embarrassed? I must be naked. Why aren't I blushing? Then I notice that he's gone. I go to the window of this room, my room. There's an aeroplane, no bigger than an insect in the sky. I go quietly back to my bed because I know the aeroplane is coming closer to me every minute and I know that Jean-Luc is on it. I felt happy for a long time after I woke up.

My mother used to bring in some embroidery with her when she came to visit me, or some crochet, but now she stares in front of her, or else she goes to the window and stares out of that. Her eyes are heavy, full of weariness.

'So why,' I hear Bella's confident voice in my mind, 'don't you put the poor old thing out of her misery and say something? It doesn't have to be brilliant. Just "Hello" would be a start.'

When I don't hear Bella, I hear Mighty Mack, who was Matron when we were in the Junior House. She had a very brisk approach to health and fitness. She was a founder-member of the 'pull-your-socks-up' school of medical treatment, and she would only provide medicines when exhortation failed. Sometimes I think: if only Mighty Mack would storm in here, clap her hands and say: 'Now, now, no more of this silly behaviour, Alice, please. A brisk walk around the lacrosse fields and a spoonful of Syrup of Figs and you'll be quite yourself again,' I would get up, dress, speak, and go about my life again. Maybe if I've failed any of my exams, I would be able to go back to school next term. But. But, but, but. What you don't know, Mighty Mack and Bella, what you have no idea of at all, is how hard I've tried.

Every morning, every single morning, I say to myself: today I'm going to get up, put on some clothes and walk out of my door and down the stairs to breakfast. And every morning I can't do it. I begin to sweat and feel faint as I think about it. By the time I reach the cupboard, my knees start trembling and my whole body sways and as I move to take a skirt from a hanger, I feel dizzy and have to go and lie down again. The truth is, I'm afraid to leave this room because the world outside my door seems threatening. I know Angus has gone. I know that he will never trouble me again, but the knowledge doesn't seem to help with the fear.

GUINÉE. 1938. Grows to fifteen feet. Darkest red of all the roses. Can seem almost black.
Guinée is curling itself over the wrought-iron gates at the bottom of the drive, lacing itself to the metal as though it were part of the design.

I eat everything my mother puts on my trays but I don't enjoy it. Often, I've forgotten in the evening what I've had to eat during the day. I just don't notice it. At Egerton Hall, my favourite food was rhubarb crumble and my best breakfast was tinned tomatoes and fried bread, but at school, of course, we thought about food a lot of the time.

'Just like in prison,' Bella used to say. Sweets and fruit sent from home were kept locked up in two cupboards just outside the Dining-Room and after lunch they were unlocked and everyone went to her labelled tin or brown paper bag and took out a little bit for that day: one apple, one orange and a bar of chocolate, say. Then great swappings would go on right up to afternoon lessons. Someone or another was always on a slimming diet and wanting to exchange a Mars bar for an apple. I often seemed to be the Prefect on Cupboard Duty. There was one more cupboard which was unlocked before supper. This one had in it whatever we wanted to spread on our bread and butter: jam or honey or Marmite or sandwich spread. Once there was a craze for chocolate spread, and another time pineapple jam was a favourite. After supper all the jars had to be locked up again.

We talked an awful lot about food, describing in detail every mouthful of the meals we'd had when our parents took us out. Things were slightly better in the Fifth and Sixth forms. We were allowed tins of biscuits in our studies, and four times a term on Saturday the Prefects gave Study Tea to a few girls from other forms. There was great competition among the Prefects to invite the pleasanter girls, and even greater competition among the lower forms to be asked to tea by someone they had a crush on. We made sandwiches and sliced cake and arranged biscuits on plates and pretended we were society hostesses. The guests came and gobbled them up and sometimes chatted happily and sometimes sat in adoring silence. Bella always had her guests in fits of laughter, imitating members of staff, or teasing Mary-Ellen, the irritating girl who shared her study.

CARDINAL RICHELIEU. Dark crimson flowers,
opening to deep purple sphere.
This grows near the summerhouse. I see it in dreams
and the flowers are almost black.

Yesterday, Aunt Lily came to see my mother. They stood at the foot of my bed and spoke as though I were not there at all. I was being lulled to sleep quite genuinely by the sound of their voices rising and falling when I suddenly heard Aunt Lily say:

'I've written to my friend Monique about poor darling Alice . . . perhaps she knows of a sanatorium in Switzerland or even Vienna. They can do such wonderful things in those continental places. They're much more sophisticated in these matters than we are. One should never give up hope.'

Oh, no, Aunt Lily, one never should! My heart leaped with the first fluttering of real joy I've had for weeks and weeks. Monique is Jean-Luc's mother. Surely if Aunt Lily tells her of my condition, she'll write and let him know, wherever he is? And surely if he knows that I'm lying here, he will come and see me? And if he does? I can't let myself hope too much. What if he thinks 'Poor Alice' and does nothing? What if he can't just drop everything and travel all the way to England?

'*Alice*,' he said to me the only time I ever saw him, '*je veux vous embrasser.*'

If he still wants to kiss me, if he wants to enough, then he'll come, however hard it may be for him. I know that if he comes, if he kisses me, I'll get up, out of this bed, out of this room, out of Arcadia House and into the world. The enchantment that has bound me here will be broken.

Aunt Lily's visit has even brought hope into a dream I had last night. I was umpiring a tennis match, something I've only done once or twice in real life. I called out the score in a loud, clear voice. Jean-Luc was playing but I can't remember who else was there. The net started growing, higher and higher, until it began to resemble a trellis with *Duchesse d'Angoulême* roses growing all over it. *Duchesse d'Angoulême* has nodding white flowers touched with very pale pink. I wanted to stop the game, but Jean-Luc kept trying to hit tennis balls over the net which now loomed above his head like a cliff.

'Game, set and match,' I called, but he continued to serve, and every time he hit one of the roses, all the petals fell to the ground.

At school, we had to do Prep. every evening, ready for the next day's lessons. I know that in day schools, pupils have to fit doing their school work into their home lives. For one thing, they have to decide when they're going to do it: should it be straight after getting home from school, or last thing at night when it becomes impossible to put it off any longer? We had all that organized for us. Special time was set aside every afternoon, and we'd sit at our desks in the J.P.R. and a prefect would sit in a big desk by the door and make sure that no one spoke and that everyone got on with their work. A girl called Janet Newsom was Head of House when we first came into the Senior School and her look was capable of turning me to stone, and not only me. Bella was always very rude about her behind her back and called her Hugebum quite openly, but somehow was always strangely quiet when Janet was taking Prep. Her bust looked to us as though it were trying to break out of her tunic and she had lots and lots of very square white teeth in an extremely pink face.

An awful lot of note-passing went on during Prep., and if the prefect was trying hard to work at her own A-level subjects, and was someone other than Janet, she used to let this pass, as long as no actual noise was made. Disruption of Prep. meant being sent out. Being sent out meant you didn't do your Prep., and if you didn't do it at the right time you had to do it during your free time, and therefore most people kept quiet. Of course, there were other ways of not doing Prep. You could write letters (me) or read books in brown paper wrappers (Bella) or write poems (Megan) but then you would get into trouble next day. We weren't very old before we decided that it was a lot less tiresome to do whatever we'd been set to do first, and go on to more enjoyable things later.

The reason I've been thinking all this is quite simple. I have to write about the party and I don't really want to. I think, I hope, that if I do write about it, as simply and clearly as I can, I shall feel as though a wound has been cleansed. Very well, then. Tomorrow I shall summon up Janet's ghostly presence and sit her in an imaginary prefect's desk in a corner of my bedroom. She will see that I don't shirk it. She will see that I get it done.

BELLE ISIS. 1845. Gallica. Pinkish-cream flowers.
Thorny stems.
This grows on the terrace. Am I imagining that the thorns seem longer, more curved, thicker on the stems now?

Three days before the party, the Aunts took up residence in the spare bedrooms. Two days before the party, vans bringing the food began to appear in the drive. A small army of men arrived one morning and started to put up huge pink and white striped marquees on the front lawn. The kitchen grew fuller and fuller of roast chickens, whole hams, sides of beef, smoked salmon and fresh salmon. Scarlet mountains of strawberries grew in the pantry, gallons of cream were beaten into snowdrifts and placed in the fridge.

'Keep well clear of Mrs Morris this morning,' Aunt May told me. 'She's making the mayonnaise and I dread to think what will become of us if it should curdle!'

So Mrs Morris was left to drip olive oil into egg yolks in the kitchen, while my mother and Aunts Myrtle, Petunia and Daisy took all the family silver out and gave it a good going over with the polish. Aunt Daisy also washed the glasses herself, thus deeply offending Mrs Moris's niece from the village who was helping out for the party and who considered it her place to be washing glasses.

Aunts Ivy, Daphne and Lily were busy with the dress. First it had to be tried on one last time, then final adjustments had to be made to the length and the fit. Then it had to be pressed very carefully indeed and left to hang outside the cupboard in my room wrapped in a long white sheet, so that no speck of dust should reach it.

Great-Aunt Hortense sat in the conservatory with a huge pot of tea and the guest list. As presents began to arrive, she would tick off the sender's name on the list and write next to it what they had sent. This was to enable me to write thank-you letters later. Here is one more thing I haven't done, one more burden for my mother. I wonder if she's written all those dozens and dozens of letters? It's something I've not thought about before.

Bella and Megan arrived on Friday afternoon, the day before the party. Aunt Daphne whisked their party dresses off to be pressed and hung up in their bedroom almost before they'd put their cases down in the hall.

Mrs Morris was icing the cake in the kitchen and the dining-room was already set for the party buffet, so for supper we had a picnic of sandwiches and salad and penguin biscuits on the terrace.

'I don't call this a proper picnic at all,' said Bella. 'No triangular cheeses.'

'You'll get a proper meal tomorrow,' said Megan, 'so stop complaining.'

'What I want to know is,' said Bella, ignoring her and biting into a beef-and-pickle doorstep, 'why all this fuss for an eighteenth birthday? Most people do this sort of thing when they're twenty-one.'

'You weren't listening when Alice told us about the malediction,' said Megan. 'This is a "let's defy Violette" party, isn't it, Alice?'

'How do you mean?' asked Bella.

'Well,' I answered, 'we're saying: here we are and I've reached eighteen with no mishaps, and just to show that we don't give a fig for curses, we're having the biggest and grandest party possible, and let's just see if any of your ill-wishing has any effect on us whatsoever.'

'Hurray!' shouted Bella. 'I get it. Pass another sandwich, Megan.'

'What about Violette, though?' Megan said. 'Has she been invited this time?'

'Oh, yes,' I nodded. 'You'll get to meet her at last, although she was a little enigmatic about when she'd be arriving. If I had to guess, I'd say, when we least expect her. Aunt Marguerite is in a frightful tizzy getting her bedroom ready. I don't think anyone wants Violette to find fault with anything.'

'Goody goody,' said Bella. 'I'm dying to see her. Has she sent you a present?'

'It's awful,' I said. 'I really hate it, only I think I shall have to wear it. It's a brooch, in the shape of a star, or a wheel or something. Anyway, it's got a lot of pointed bits sticking out all over the place, and what's more it's studded all over with tiny opals, which are dreadfully unlucky.'

'Do you have to wear it?' Megan asked. 'At the party I mean. Can't you say it doesn't go with your dress?'

I shook my head. 'We can't risk it. Even Aunt Daphne says so, and you can see how much it upsets her that the outfit she's been planning for so long won't be perfect in every detail. "We shall just," she says, "have to grin and bear it. It won't be too bad. We will pin it on to your sash. Just by the bow and then the bow will almost hide it. Oh, how typical of Violette to provide flies for any ointment she can get her hands on!"'

'I simply can't wait for tomorrow,' said Bella, stretching out on the grass and turning her face to the sun. 'I just adore getting ready for parties. That's the best bit of the whole thing. What time can we start?'

'Oh, first thing in the morning,' I said. 'We've got to do all the hairwashing and setting and things.'

'Not me,' said Megan. 'I hardly even have to comb mine. But I'll help both of you with your rollers and things if you like.'

'Now, Megan, don't be offended,' said Bella, 'but Aunt Lily is in charge of Hair. She is personally overseeing every curl and ringlet . . . oh, I can't wait! I shall be able to spend an entire day titivating.'

'I can't think,' said Megan, 'of anything more boring.'

'Wet blanket! Killjoy!' Bella began to pelt Megan with bits of pulled-up grass. 'Off you go to the conservatory and read a book or something if you don't want to chat to us while we're getting ready.'

'I never said I didn't want to chat,' Megan said soothingly. 'Just that it was boring to titivate all day long.'

'Well,' said Bella, 'I've raided Marjorie's dressing-table and brought along every cream and unguent I could find. We'll have such good fun! I wish it could be tomorrow right now!'

Bella was quite right. Getting ready for the party turned out to be wonderful. Speculating about how we would look, whom we would dance with, what they would say, was like imagining all our best dreams.

'It'll have to be a pretty amazing party,' said Bella, 'if it's going to live up to expectations.'

The day started with very long, highly-perfumed baths for all of us. We each bathed in turn, and whoever wasn't actually in the water was there simply to chat, so the whole process took ages.

'It's exactly like the Junior House all over again,' said Megan. 'Remember how we used to bath in groups of three?'

'I hated it,' I said, 'but I like this.'

'And we don't have to worry about modesty,' said Megan. 'Bella's bath has made such a fog in here, I can scarcely find the sink.'

'It's steam,' said Bella, who was almost completely submerged. 'Marjorie says it's awfully good for the complexion. It opens the pores and lets the skin breathe.'

'I like my pores just as they are, thank you,' I said. 'All this steam's making me feel so sweaty, I shall need another bath.'

At last, everyone was clean and powdered and had every pore they possessed thoroughly opened.

'And our fingers and toes,' Bella added, 'look like white prunes.'

We all went to my room. Aunt Lily then glided in and began fiddling with rollers and kirby grips and setting lotions. Bella, almost before she had sat down at the dressing-table, started to ask Aunt Lily all the questions I'd been too embarrassed to ask for days.

'Why isn't Alice's boyfriend coming tonight? You know, Jean-Luc, the son of your friend.'

'Alice's boyfriend?' Aunt Lily paused, tail comb quivering in her hand. 'They only met once in my house, as far as I know, and that was last year.'

'But didn't you know they'd been writing to one another?' Bella asked.

'No.' Aunt Lily resumed winding Bella's black hair on to enormous rollers. 'Alice, you naughty little thing! Why ever didn't you tell me? I wonder if Monique has any idea . . .?'

'No, really, Aunt Lily,' I said hastily. 'He's not really my boyfriend. Bella's exaggerating as per usual. I've just been writing to him now and then. It's very helpful to me' (oh, this was a brilliant idea! How quick of me, I thought, to summon it up at this moment!) 'for my written French.'

'Yes, I suppose it must be,' said Aunt Lily, losing interest now that Romance had been reduced to less than fairytale proportions.

'But still,' (Bella never could leave well enough alone and she continued her interrogation of Aunt Lily undeterred) 'he could have been invited. He is a friend of Alice's and hundreds and hundreds of people are coming she's never even laid eyes on before. He might have sent her a card or a present.'

'I'm sure he has,' I said, not feeling sure at all. 'I mean I did write and tell him. And I invited him to the party. It's just that sometimes things take ages to come from Africa, or even get lost in the post.'

'Fancy having to go all the way to Africa for your military service!' said Bella. 'It is a bit of a long way to come just for a party, I suppose. Oh, well,' Bella's glance met mine in the mirror, 'you'll just have to keep your eyes peeled tonight, and see what you can find.'

'Ugh!' Megan shivered. 'What a disgusting expression! Imagine having your eyes peeled. It's dreadful!'

'Right, Bella, you're finished,' said Aunt Lily. 'You next, Alice. Come and sit down here.'

I went and sat in front of the mirror and Aunt Lily began to divide my hair into dozens of sections waiting to be rolled up. I was to have it done on top of my head in some kind of knot, from which a waterfall of ringlets would tumble on to my bare shoulders. I peered at myself, trying to imagine what it would look like. Bella and Megan had been diverted for a while into a discussion about the staying-up powers of the strapless bra, so I was left alone to wonder who, indeed, if Jean-Luc were not here, would make the party a pleasant one for me.

SISSINGHURST CASTLE. Old Gallica. Dark red.
This rose has become entangled in the small gate of the kitchen garden, winding itself in and out of the spirals and scrolls of the black wrought iron. The edges of the petals are blighted.

The afternoon passed. We lounged about in our dressing-gowns, watching the chairs and tables being set out on the terrace.

'How divine!' Bella said. 'We get our food from the dining room and bring it out there. Lovely. Like something from a film.'

I saw my father walking about among the roses with Mr Harris, making sure that every flower was at its best. I knew that that morning, even before Megan, Bella and I had woken up, he'd been out picking hundreds of buds that were just on the point of opening. They were now arranged in vases all over the house. Now he was making sure that all the fallen petals had been swept up, and that any rose that showed the slightest sign of decay was snipped off and thrown away.

At about six o'clock, we began to put on our make-up. Bella was in charge of that.

'O.K. Megan, you first,' she said.

'Now don't go overboard,' Megan protested. 'Truly, I'll look fine with a bit of lipstick and just some powder to take the shine off my nose.'

'Shut up,' said Bella. 'You just have no idea how wonderful you'll look when I've finished with you.'

Megan didn't shut up. She moaned and complained like a child in a dentist's chair. Every now and then there'd be a wailing:

'Oh, Bella, not foundation! Why do I have to have that?' or 'That eyeshadow's too green' or 'You're hurting me . . . what if that brush goes in my eye?'

Bella didn't even bother to reply. In the end she said:

'There you are, Megan, take a look. And don't you dare to contradict me ever again.'

Megan looked. She grinned at Bella.

'Humble and grovelling apologies, oh wondrous miracle worker! Truly, I am transformed.'

She was. It was the first time I had ever seen Megan looking beautiful. She hurried away to put on her sea-coloured dress.

'You next, Alice,' said Bella, 'then me.'

'But I won't be able to tell how I look,' I said, 'because of the rollers.'

'Yes, you will,' said Bella. 'Aunt Lily is arriving to arrange the tresses in twenty minutes, so we'd better get cracking. I'm going to need ages and ages if I'm to look half as good as you and Megan.'

I try not to look in my mirror any more, because what I see there frightens me. I think: this is what I shall be like when I am dead. This is how my skin will be: grey and lifeless. My eyes will have these purple smudges all round them, and my hair will hang down sadly on either side of my face. All my life everyone has told me I am beautiful. I never truly believed them. Looking at myself today, I can see that I was right all along. On the night of the party, though, I came very close to beauty. Bella had put blue eyeshadow on my eyelids, and brushed the lashes with mascara. My lipstick was exactly the colour of the rose called *Celeste* and my cheeks glowed with what Bella called 'the merest whisper of rouge'. Aunt Lily had arranged my hair, and every separate ringlet caught the light.

'It looks,' said Megan, 'like burnished gold.'

'What it is to be a poet!' Bella said. 'I was just going to say it looked terrific.'

'And you both look terrific, too,' I said, and they did. 'Megan, you look like a proper sea-nymph and Bella, you look like . . . like . . .'

'Like Carmen!' said Bella and began to improvise a flamenco dance. 'Only I can't do this dance on such a thick carpet. Just wait till we get downstairs. Olé!'

Bella's dress was scarlet, with a skirt shaped like a tulip. 'I wanted flounces in tiers,' she said, 'and a black lace mantilla and comb, but Marjorie said it would be altogether too much.'

'Well,' I said, 'you look wonderful just as you are.' Bella's eyes shone. 'Oh, I know I do,' she said. 'Anyone I get my little mitts on had better watch out. I feel positively dangerous. It's only a bit of a disappointment to me, Alice, that your parents didn't invite Pete and the band to provide the music. Then I could have sung in front of all your guests.'

'Knowing you,' Megan said, 'you probably will anyway.'

By the time I put my dress on, everyone else was ready. They gathered in my bedroom: Megan and Bella, my mother and most of the Aunts, and Miss van der Leyden. I felt like a mannequin in a window, being dressed for a display. No one said anything while the zip was fastened at the back, while the sash was tied and Violette's brooch pinned next to the bow. No one even dared to breathe, it seemed to me. Aunt Daphne fiddled with the lace of the skirt, pulled the satin sash a little to the left, and then stood back rather like (Megan said later) Michelangelo after he'd put the finishing touches to his statue of David. Everyone breathed again. Little shrieks of delight and exclamations of wonder rose into the air. My mother came towards me with tears in her eyes and kissed me. Megan and Bella hugged me and jumped up and down.

'You are without doubt,' said Bella, 'the Belly of the Ball.'

'"Belle", dear,' said Great-Aunt Hortense, 'to rhyme with "tell". Not "belly."'

'Oh, I know,' said Bella. 'It was supposed to be a joke.'

Great-Aunt Hortense looked at her without any sign of comprehension.

'Never mind,' Bella said. 'Alice looks wonderful. That's all I was trying to say.'

CRAMOISI SUPÉRIEUR. Climber. Red flowers in clusters.
The stems now form a closely-woven trellis outside the dining-room window, and the flowers look like spreading bloodstains.

*

For the first hour of my party, I felt as though I'd been transported to a magic realm that looked like the inside of a kaleidoscope. Every time I moved, every time I turned my head, the house, the guests, the jewels, the flowers, and the music shifted and settled into different patterns, each one more entrancing than the last. My hand was weak from being shaken, and I was dizzy from smiling and kissing and walking between one knot of people and another and thanking them for their wonderful gifts. The sunlight of early evening was still coming through the open windows, throwing ribbons of gold around the gigantic tubs of roses that stood in every corner.

'I don't know,' said Bella, 'how we're ever going to investigate the possibility of divine young men with this circus going on.'

'Aunt Myrtle says it'll thin out a bit later,' I said, 'when people go out into the garden and when they realize that there are drinks and music in the marquees.'

'I need a drink,' said Bella. 'I still haven't quite recovered from meeting the dreaded Violette.'

We giggled with relief that at least one ordeal was over. Violette had been standing with the other aunts in a corner of the drawing-room when my mother took me over to be introduced. Megan and Bella stayed close behind me. Violette was dressed in a dark purple robe that looked, Bella said later, like an exceedingly posh dressing-gown. When she kissed me, her lips were cool and a chilly draught seemed to spring up from her skirts and blow along my bare arms and shoulders, so that I was immediately covered in gooseflesh.

'You've turned out,' she said to me, 'exactly as I had expected . . .' and she laughed. 'I regret I cannot stay to see,' she smiled, 'how the party ends.' She turned to my father. 'You have cultivated here, William, a rose among roses. One that is ready, more than ready, to be plucked.' Then she raised one hand in the air and held it for a moment a few inches from my face in a scissor-shape.

'Snip, snip, snip,' she said and let out a thin, metallic sort of laugh. 'Oh, most assuredly, snip, snip, snip.'

The rays of the dying sun flashed white light from the rings on her fingers, and lit up her whole hand so that for one dreadful second – no, less than a second: a tiny instant of time but one that I remember now as though it had been branded on my vision – her arm seemed to end in a pair of giant scissors with their points ready to cut into my skin. Then the moment passed and everything was different.

Violette left soon afterwards, in a sweep of purple. A shiny, black car with darkened glass at the windows made its way up the drive. We watched it pulling up at the front door, Megan, Bella and I, from one of the drawing-room windows. Violette folded herself into the car, and it went down the drive again and disappeared. Everyone else was much too busy enjoying themselves to take much notice.

'When, though,' said Bella, 'did she arrive? I never saw her and your parents never mentioned it. Nor did the Aunts.'

'I don't know,' I said. 'She always seems to appear. And disappear. She sort of swoops down like a bird.'

'She *is* like a bird,' said Megan. 'Tall and beaky and with those dark eyes.'

'A kind of purple stork,' said Bella. 'Or an oversized crow or raven.' She laughed. 'But her eyes were strange. Did you notice, Alice?'

'Notice what?'

'That the pupils were almost yellow,' Bella said. 'I don't expect they were really. I should think it was just a trick of the light, but still, it gave me the shivers.'

Megan nodded. 'At least we know now why she's called "the dreaded Violette". I'm jolly glad she's gone. Now we can get on and enjoy the rest of the party.'

And, at first, I did enjoy the party, just as I had been expecting to. Bella ate too many strawberries. We went about making rude remarks to one another about other people's dresses.

'The Egerton Hall contingent,' said Bella, 'looks quite good on the whole, only I *do* think Roberta's lime green is a mistake, and why is Fiona wearing a sort of tartan scarf over her dress like an Order of the Garter?'

'It's because she's Scottish,' Megan said.

'No excuse,' said Bella. 'No excuse at all. I can't actually think why you invited all these people.'

'I had to invite someone,' I said, 'so I invited friends from school.'

'And lots of other people too,' Bella said, 'but Male Divinities are a little thin on the ground.'

'I don't know all that many boys,' I said. 'Most of these are from Aunt Lily's list of eligible young men about town.'

Bella sighed. 'They're all so respectable. So well-scrubbed. I'd like to meet someone really rascally and scandalous and flirt like mad. I think I'll go and make friends with the band.'

Bella walked off towards one of the marquees.

That was the last time I saw Bella to speak to. Later on in the evening, I heard her singing 'Moon River' with the band my father had hired to play for dancing. My attention was elsewhere at the time, and I had had a few glasses of punch, but I can remember thinking what a beautiful song it was and how Bella's voice suited it, streaming into the warm night like moonlight. Moon river, I thought fuzzily, such a lovely name . . . so lovely, so sweet.

I ask myself now, I have asked myself for weeks on end a question to which there is no answer: how was it that I didn't recognize Angus? How was it that the face that had filled my nightmares didn't immediately set off all kinds of alarm bells in me? Maybe it did. Maybe what I felt when I saw him standing under one of the apple trees – and I hadn't noticed him before – was a thrill of fear and I didn't realize that that was what it was. I have gone over and over this in my mind. I have gone round and round a central question until I am almost mad with uncertainty. The question I cannot answer is this: was it my fault? Was anything that happened my fault? I know it wasn't. They tell me again and again that it wasn't. My mother has clearly been advised by the doctor, told that she must emphasize this, must convince me of my own innocence, and when she sits by my bed, she recites like a poem, like a kind of lullaby:

'It wasn't your fault, Alice.
Nothing was your fault.
Nothing that happened to you was your fault.'

I believe her. Most of the time, I believe her, and yet I keep thinking: if only. If only I had recognized him. If only I had known. If only: the saddest words in the world.

He was different, quite different from what I remembered. He was very tall and strong and dark. You couldn't see his broad shoulders and muscles under the dinner-jacket, but you could tell they were there. His hands were hairy at the wrists, his eyebrows nearly met over his nose. His teeth were white and pointed in a longish face, but his mouth no longer hung open. Does he sound a little like a wolf? I suppose that I am not giving an unbiased description. If I'm honest, I have to admit I thought him handsome when I saw him. Dangerous looking. A little wild about the eyes, but definitely handsome. I felt angry that Jean-Luc had not even sent me a letter for my eighteenth birthday. I felt defiant. I felt a little giggly and silly because I'd had some punch. I felt I should be grown-up and flirt a little, and most of all (and I know this was a very peculiar sentiment in the middle of a party in my honour, a party crowded with my friends) I felt completely alone. Everywhere I looked there were couples dancing, talking, laughing, eating and I was on my own. Bella was singing and Megan had gone off with Marion Tipton and her boyfriend to find some more food.

Angus walked towards me across the grass. He came straight up to me. As he walked, he looked at me and I stood frozen, mesmerized until he was right beside me.

'May I,' he said, 'have the pleasure of this dance, Alice?'

I shivered slightly as my name was spoken. Did I hear echoes of long-ago hissing? That's what I think now. At the time I thought: the evening is losing its warmth a little.

'I don't think I know you,' I whispered.

'Of course not. How awfully rude of me. I'm Andrew Green. I came with the Hendersons.'

One of the names, I thought, from Aunt Lily's list of London Eligibles.

'How do you know my name?' I asked.

'You were pointed out as the birthday girl. It's an awful cheek on my part, I know, asking you to dance when there must be hordes of people clamouring to partner you, but you've been standing on your own for a while, so I thought I'd try my luck.'

He smiled and I felt a kind of squeezing around my heart. I thought I might be blushing. I said:

'There are no hordes at the moment. I'd love to dance.'

We went into the marquee where the music was. I haven't often danced with a man. At school, it's always girls we practise on, during dancing lessons or the frightful Saturday Night Dancing. Andrew – Angus – felt strange. I was aware of how hard his body was under the suit. Heat seemed to flow from it. His hand holding mine seemed enormous. He towered over me. If I looked up and sideways I could see the line of his jaw, which was dark with the beginnings of a beard.

We paused between dances. I was hot from being so close to him. I drank more fruit punch, which tasted cool and sweet but which also made me silly and muddled in the head. If only. There I go again. If only I hadn't had quite so much fruit punch.

I relaxed. Instead of standing stiffly in the circle of Angus's arm, keeping my distance, not touching him except where I absolutely had to, I leaned into his body, felt myself dissolving round the edges. He said things into my ear, told me how beautiful I was, how soft, how white, how lovely, and all the time drew me closer and closer to him.

I could have stopped it. I could have pulled myself away. I could have run into the house, made an excuse, danced with someone else and I didn't. I liked it. There, I've said it and I feel as if I've dug out a splinter of wood that's been under my nail for a very long time. I liked it. Was I wrong to like it? Did my liking it give Angus some excuse for how he treated me later? I know, deep in my heart, that it didn't, but still the worry persists. I say: I liked it. That's a very bad way of describing how I felt and not quite true. I liked it and I hated it. I wanted it and was terrified by it all at once. I felt as if I were on a rollercoaster: I wanted to scream and be sick, my stomach felt as though it were going to fly out of my mouth, but I didn't want it to stop.

After many dances, we stepped outside the marquee. The night was starlit all around us. I could smell the roses. Angus kissed me quite softly on the mouth.

'Alice,' he whispered, 'where can we go? I want to be alone with you.'

He touched my hair and kissed me again. My heart was beating very fast. I felt dizzy and hot and a little ill.

'We can go to the summerhouse,' I said. My voice sounded thick and fuzzy to me.

'Then let's go there,' Angus said, and took my hand. As we walked down the gravel paths, people passed us. I heard the rustling of skirts coming towards me, vanishing behind me into the darkness. It was just as if they were ghosts: misty, insubstantial shapes drifting to the strains of music that came from a very long way off. My legs felt wobbly. Angus put an arm round me to help me.

'You'll feel better sitting down,' he said.

We followed the path across the back lawns, and made our way to the summerhouse. I went in first. There's a round, wrought-iron table in there and chairs with cushions on them. I sat down on one of these, suddenly feeling very weak. Away from the marquee lights, Angus was nothing but a black shape against the glass. I felt a moment of pure terror as he shut the door behind him. I closed my eyes. When I opened them, he was kneeling beside me, his head almost on a level with mine, but a little lower, so that I touched his hair with my mouth when I turned my face.

'Alice,' he murmured, 'oh, Alice, Alice please . . . please kiss me, Alice.'

He buried his face in my shoulder, saying my name over and over again. It was then, at that moment, that I realized exactly who he was.

I don't know how to write about what happened to me in the summerhouse. All these days of lying here, of writing everything down and saying nothing to anyone, I have dreaded this moment. I knew it would come. I would have to open a door, like a cupboard door in my head which I have kept very firmly shut, and look again at the monstrous thing hiding there in the dark. Sometimes I've thought: I can avoid it. I can exorcise it in one sentence. I can be brief, factual and to the point, like a police report: At approximately twelve midnight on the night of June 20th, the accused (for I like to think of him as in the dock, though he will never appear there) raped one Alice Gregson (18) of Arcadia House. There, I've written it and I hate it. It's a word that gives me pain when I think it, sears the page as I write, leaves a trail of anguish and sorrow in my heart when I think it – and which sounds like fingernails scraping a blackboard. But writing that sentence isn't enough. I need to go through it, at least the parts of it that I remember.

As soon as I knew who he was, I became ice-cold and began to shiver. The part of my brain that was still working properly said: be calm. You're no longer a child. Speak firmly to him. Apologize. Say you want to go back to the house. Be quite friendly, but make it clear that you're no longer interested. Talk your way out of this. Disarm him. Distract him. Suggest going to dance a little more. Finally, I said:

'I know who you are, you know.'

He laughed: 'When did you realize?'

'Only a moment ago. You've changed an awful lot.'

'I know. You'd never have danced with me if you'd known who I was. Go on. Admit it.'

(Lie, said a voice in my head. Be light. Be frivolous. Pretend you're Bella.)

'I don't know . . .' (fading away.)

'I do. Wouldn't come near me when we were kids.'

'You . . . you frightened me. You were so rough.'

'You don't mind that now, though.'

(Keep your voice full of laughter) 'You're not rough now. You're jolly sophisticated.' (Flatter him. Placate him.) 'And a jolly good dancer. In fact,' I stood up and pushed the chair away a little, 'I'd like to dance with you again. Shall we go back to the marquee?'

He laughed. It sounded like a growl in this throat.

'Oh, no, you're not getting away that easily. Oh no.'

'Why?' My voice sounded high and shrill in my ears. A squeak. A pathetic little mouse-squeak. 'What would you like to do? Would you like some food? There's strawberries.'

'I'd like,' he said, coming closer, gathering me in his arms, 'to nibble on you a little. Gobble you all up.'

I pulled away from him but his arms were strong, wouldn't loosen their grip.

'But I don't feel like . . .' I began. He laughed again, that hideous laugh that had nothing at all of pleasure or fun in it, only a threat of anger in it somewhere, a promise of pain.

'You didn't mind before,' he said. 'In fact, I got the impression you quite liked it. You're not going to turn out to be a little teaser, are you?'

'I don't know what you mean,' I stammered. 'I don't know what a teaser is. But I'm not one. I'm positive I'm not. No one's ever called me that before.'

'A teaser,' he said, 'is *exactly* what you are. You lead a chap on, and you flirt and toss your curls and smile and press yourself against him soft as a lamb, and you're happy to kiss him and maybe even let him touch you – above the waist, mind – but that's it. Not a step further. Well, that might work with the milksops you're used to, but I'm different.'

He smiled at me then . . . I could see his teeth in the light from the stars, and his breath burned my cheeks. I thought: I could scream. I will scream. Someone will come if I scream and take him away. I'll imagine he's a horrible hairy spider, that's all, and if I scream loudly enough, someone will hear and come and pluck him off my body.

I screamed. I screamed as loudly as I knew how. I didn't know, I never realized that there was so much sound inside me. But I shouldn't have screamed. It was a mistake. It made him very angry and he slapped me. He slapped me in the face. I cried out with the pain and fell back into the chair. He stood over me.

'I really shouldn't do that if I were you, Alice. No one will hear you, for a start, because we're so far from the house, and there's all that music and laughter, isn't there? Besides which, if you scream, I shall have to do something I'd really hate to do and which you'd hate as well. So don't make me, there's a good girl.'

'What,' I whispered, 'what will you do?'

His eyes glittered. He put his face close to mine and said:

'I'll cut you. I've got a razor in my pocket and I'll cut your pretty face. You wouldn't like that, Alice, now would you?'

'No.' I was beginning to freeze up, to turn to stone, starting at my feet. I closed my eyes, so that I shouldn't have to see him. I tried to think of myself as not being there, as being out of my body, as not being real. I tried to imagine I was not a person, but a marble statue. I tried to think: it'll all be over soon. Keep still and it'll all be over soon. If you keep still and don't move, he can't hurt you. Just keep still.

I kept still. I closed my eyes – oh, but I could still smell him and feel him: his hands crawling over my skin, his breathing coming faster and faster, rasping in his throat. He tore off my satin sash, and pulled me to my feet. I'm a rag-doll, I thought. I'm a nothing, a non-person. I flopped, lifeless in his arms. He laid me down on the concrete floor and it was hard and cold on my back. He lay down alongside me, breathing on me. His hands pushed at my dress. I felt his fingers close over my breasts. Then he pulled at my skirts. I heard tearing. I thought: I want to die. Please God let me die. Let me die now before anything else happens.

I didn't die then. I died later. I died as his full weight rolled on to me, died as I felt him crush me and cover my mouth with his, stopping the sounds that I could hear coming from me in spite of myself: the thin, bloodstained shrieks of a small animal in the teeth of a metal trap.

*

I must have fainted, I suppose. When I came to, I was alone in the summerhouse, on the dirty, concrete floor. After a long time, I sat up. My breasts were bare. I touched them and they were sore. My mouth felt bruised and swollen. When I looked down at my legs I burst into tears and was glad that it was dark. My knickers were still around one ankle. The skirt of my dress was torn. So were my stockings. My thighs were covered in slime, as though slugs had crawled over my flesh, leaving trails of blood. I don't know how long I sat there. Then I stood up. I could stand. I pulled my knickers on again and tried to find my sash, feeling about for it all over the floor. I found it in the end, but Violette's brooch must have sprung open and I pricked my finger on the pin. I held my hand against my skirt to stop the pain, and when I took it away I noticed the small spots of darkness my blood was making on the fabric. Help, I thought. I must get help. My mother. My father. Bella. Megan. I couldn't bear the thought of seeing anyone. I wanted silent, unquestioning, undemanding comfort. I staggered into the garden thinking: I'll go and find Miss van der Leyden. I found it hard to walk. I felt like a butterfly, pierced through the core by a metal pin. Impaled.

VIRIDIFLORA (montrosa.) 1843. Permanently deformed flowers. Petals: green scales, later tinged with red.
My father told me that this rose is a botanical freak, a curiosity. It grows hidden among the trees in the orchard.

The steps to Miss van der Leyden's room go round and round in a spiral. The light there is very dim. I could see my own shadow walking at my side. My long skirt, spread out behind me, looked like black wings on the wall. Miss van der Leyden was surprised to see me. She had already got into her bed, and when I came in, she got up and went behind a small screen that stood near the washbasin, to put her dressing-gown on, I think. As she was doing that, she chattered away: why was I leaving the party, she asked, and did I want tea . . . would I sit for a minute . . . and how sweet, how kind of me to spare a thought for a sick old woman when there was all that revelry going on below. I must have answered. I must have made some replies that seemed quite sensible, because otherwise she would have come out sooner from behind the screen. I can remember leaning against the chest-of-drawers. My thumb had begun to bleed again where Violette's brooch had pricked me. When Miss van der Leyden turned at last and saw me, her hand flew to her mouth and she screamed.

'*Alice, ma petite,*' she sobbed, '*qu'est-ce qu'il-y-a? Oh, quelle horreur!*'

Her voice was like a bell that woke me up.

'It was a man . . . Angus,' I muttered. 'He . . .' I couldn't go on, but what I had said was enough. I could see from her face, from the way it was dissolving, melting with anguish, that she knew, that she could guess what had happened. Suddenly, I found I couldn't bear it. I ran for the door and tore it open. Then I raced down the spiral staircase, down through the kitchen, out of the back door and into the garden. If only, I thought, I could get to the orchard, I could lose myself among the trees and no one would find me.

No one came looking for me for a long time. Miss van der Leyden, I learned later from my mother, had collapsed on the night of the party. She had, my mother said, fallen down the stairs. It must have been Miss van der Leyden who told my parents what she had learned, and even more importantly, the identity of the person responsible for the state I was in.

I don't know how long I spent in the orchard. I leaned against one tree after another. Roses grew round every single one of them, and I knew it. I simply wanted the thorns to hurt me. They made small holes in the fabric of my dress, tiny pinpricks in the skin of my chest and arms. I wanted some pain to distract me from what had happened, to take my mind over, to stop me thinking . . . thinking. I don't know why I went back to the summerhouse, but I remember wanting to destroy something, someone. I wanted to hurt. I wanted to cut and tear apart. The summerhouse was empty, of course. Someone had left a pair of shears there, though, and that was where they found me. I don't know how long I'd been there. I was cutting up the cushions into small pieces with the garden shears. I shall never forget my father's face when he saw me. I think they had been looking for me for hours. Even in the orchard, I think I heard my name being called. My father picked me up and brought me to this room. The party was over.

HEBE'S LIP. 1912. Damask. Semi-double flowers.
Cream edged with crimson. Flowers close at night.
This rose grows in a round bed on the back lawn. The
dark edges of the petals seem dipped in blood.

At first, you say nothing because even forming the thoughts that are in your head into real words is terribly painful. Then you say nothing because you are protecting someone: your parents, everyone who loves you. You think: if I tell them this, they will think I am different, worse, defiled in some way. Then you say nothing because you've fallen into the habit of not speaking and it's easy to let a crust of silence form like a scab over a bleeding wound.

But writing this is a kind of talking and I feel: if only I had done it straight away, poured all the poison out at once, to my parents, Bella, Megan, then I would never have needed to lie here all these weeks under my blanket of misery.

At school, people were forever having poultices put on boils by Mighty Mack. Mighty Mack believed in poultices.

'They draw all the horrid substances out of the body, d'ye see,' she said, 'and leave the sore place empty and clean, ready to heal all by itself.'

That is how I feel now, having rid myself at last of this burden: empty and clean and ready to heal.

Everything will heal. That's what my mother said and maybe she's right. This morning I spoke. My voice sounded very peculiar, like a rusty hinge. I went to the mirror and stood in front of it. Then I said, 'Hello, Alice,' and a thin, pale stranger with wild red curls stared at me out of uncomprehending eyes and seemed to say, 'Hello, Alice,' at the same time. I was just thinking: 'I'll walk out now, walk downstairs to my mother, speak to her, tell her I'm feeling better . . . and then I heard my mother's tread on the stairs, and I fled back to my bed, to rearrange myself into the patterns of sleep she'd grown used to. I felt so angry with myself, so disappointed that I wasn't really better, that I nearly cried, all over again.

My mother said: 'Alice, Alice, if you can hear me, I've got news that will make you happy. A parcel came for you today. All the way from Africa. It's taken simply ages and ages, but here it is at last . . . a birthday present from your French pen-friend. It's very pretty. I'll put it here, on the bedside table with the letter . . .' She went on and on talking, and I waited for her to finish, and leave the room so that I could see what it was that Jean-Luc had sent me. He hadn't forgotten me. He hadn't forgotten my birthday. Oh, go, please go, I said silently in my head to my mother, over and over again. Please, please go.

When she left, I picked up Jean-Luc's present. It was a small antelope carved from a wood that shone like brown-yellow satin. The letter was not a letter, but more of a note:

'Heureux Anniversaire, ma chère Alice! Je ne pense qu'à toi. À bientôt. Jean-Luc.'

*

Je ne pense qu'à toi . . . I'm thinking only of you. *À bientôt* . . . see you soon. It was, I thought, a strange thing to put in a note. It was more the kind of thing you say to someone when you're going to see them tomorrow, or next week . . . Soon. Very soon.

BOURBON QUEEN. 1834. Pink and white clusters.
Free flowering.
This rose, growing at the back of the house, has so
much massed blossom this year that it looks like a
cloud at sunrise, touched with new colour.

I haven't written in these pages for three days. There has been no time. Arcadia House is waking up, coming back to life again. The dust sheets have been taken off the furniture. My mother hasn't played the piano, not yet, but she has dusted and polished it and put back all the photographs that used to stand on it. I have seen her looking at it with longing. She will play it soon, just as soon as Arcadia House is back to normal. Mrs Morris is back in the kitchen. There is a new daily from Egerton Parva who dusts and polishes all day long. Curtains have been taken down and sent to the cleaners, and the hum of the Hoover fills the corridors. My father is not to be seen. He is in the garden from morning till night, tidying the roses, nursing them back to health, watering them, feeding them, cutting off all the dead heads, the tangled stems, the neglected, overgrown thorns. He has three men to help him.

I feel as though my life has begun again. Jean-Luc is here. He and I walk through the gardens. I have told him everything. I have spoken on the telephone to Megan and Bella. They have special permission from Miss Herbert to come and stay here next weekend. We have all passed our exams. When I heard the news, I had to think for a good few seconds before I remembered exactly what the word meant. I have 'B' for Art and English and 'C' for French. Bella has 'A' for English and French and 'B' for Spanish. Megan, naturally, has all 'A's. They are both back in Egerton Hall.

'You come back too, Alice,' Megan said. 'It'll be such fun. We could get the Tower Room again. I'm sure we could, if you came back. It's only for the University entrance.'

'No,' I said. 'I couldn't bear it. Not more exams. Not now. I'll come and visit you both. I'll take you out to The Old Forge.'

'What about University?' Megan said.

'I don't want to go to University. Not at the moment.'

Bella said: 'What will you do? We've been so worried, honestly, Alice. They wouldn't let us write. They said you were in a coma. Is that true. Were you?'

'In a way. I suppose a kind of coma. I don't know what I'll do. Go to France, perhaps, to meet Jean-Luc's family.'

'Lucky thing!' Bella cried. 'I've been in Paris almost the whole of the hols. It was fantastic, honestly! I can't wait to tell you about it. However did Jean-Luc arrive like that out of the blue? Were you expecting him?'

'I wasn't expecting anyone. Aunt Lily had told his mother and she had written to him. The army has given him special compassionate leave, just so that he could come. He'll have to go back in the end, of course, but not for ages yet. Not until Christmas.'

'How wonderful! Only are you O.K. now? Really?'

'I'm fine. I'll tell you everything when you arrive. I can't wait to see you both.'

I will tell them. I will also give them this notebook to read and because of that, I have left Jean-Luc talking to my father in the garden and come up to my room to finish the story.

The day after Jean-Luc's present arrived, I woke up very

early and stood beside my window for a long time, noticing how autumn had begun to creep into the sunlight, turning the first leaves on the trees, blowing the first frosty mists into the pale daylight. In the early morning noise carries a very long way. I heard a distant metallic shaking, like chains being pulled about, and I couldn't think what it was. I looked all round the garden and saw nothing. I opened my window to get a better view and the rattling iron noise was louder. It's someone rattling at the gates, I thought. Why are they doing that? I looked round the drive to see what was happening and the rattling stopped. Then I saw a head sticking up over the top of the gates. Someone was climbing over them. It's a burglar, I thought. It's someone come to rob us. Immediately, though, I knew it couldn't be a burglar. What thief in his right mind would rattle and shake the gates and then climb over them in broad daylight? The person started to walk up the drive. Then he stepped on to the lawns below the terrace and I recognized Jean-Luc. He made his way up to the house, through the overgrown roses. I could see him stepping over stems, pushing his way through the creeping tendrils of plants that had run wild into a mesh of green twigs, and crushing under his feet the fallen petals from flowers that had once been pink and red and cream and crimson, and were now turning into snowdrifts of a uniform faded beige.

When Jean-Luc reached the porch, I hid behind a curtain so that he shouldn't see me. The door was locked, of course. He knocked and knocked and no one came to open it. I saw him hesitate beside the hall window. It was open just a little at the bottom. The beigey-pink flowers and thorny stems of *La Vesuve* had crept over the sill. Jean-Luc carefully pulled them back and away from the wall. He looked around him. Could he feel my eyes following him? I jumped back into the room, the beats of my own heart very loud in my head. Then

I heard the noise of the window being pushed up, the squeak of the stiff wood. I lay down on the bed and closed my eyes. I thought: this must be a dream. Nothing is what it seems in a dream. In a moment, I shall wake up and none of it will have been true. I could hear Jean-Luc's voice now, calling softly for me.

'*Alice! Alice, òu es-tu? Alice, c'est moi. C'est Jean-Luc.*'

I tried to imagine where he was. Suddenly, I heard his footsteps on the stairs. I could feel him gently opening and closing all the doors along this corridor. I flew to the bed and lay down, arranging myself with my hands folded over my heart. Then he opened the door of my bedroom and silence fell all over the house. Did it take him two seconds or three to cross the carpet to my bed? To me those seconds stretched and stretched so that I could hardly bear the waiting. My eyes were closed, but I could smell him. He smelled of the garden, and damp cloth.

'*Alice,*' he whispered, kneeling down beside the bed. '*Alice, enfin* . . . wake up, it's me. It's Jean-Luc.'

'I know it's you,' I said, opening my eyes. 'I've been looking at you. Out of the window. I saw you climb over the gate.'

'I did not know how to come in,' he said. His eyes were even bluer than I remembered. 'But I knew I needed to see you, and now,' he blushed and looked away, 'now that I have arrived, I have nothing to say. I do not know what to say.'

'It doesn't matter,' I said. 'You don't have to say anything. I'm very happy . . . happy to see you.'

'Alice . . .' he said, and stood up and went over to the window so that I could no longer see his face. 'Alice . . . my mother has told me what happened to you. If I could pick up, carry away some of your pain, I would do it.'

'It's all right,' I said. 'Just seeing you again makes it all right. Don't let's talk about horrid things.'

He came over to the bed and sat down on it just in the way that Dr Benyon often sat. He took my hand.

'*Alice,*' he whispered, '*je veux te donner un baiser.*'

What silly things come into your head sometimes! What I was saying to myself at that moment was: he must like me. Last time he said that, I was '*vous*' and he's not using the more formal '*embrasser*'. Oh, he must like me a lot. Even after all this time. He thinks I am someone worth climbing gates and creeping through windows for, someone for whom he is prepared to tear roses from the sills, someone worth searching for.

He kissed me then.

Sometimes, when the weather turns hot, the roses need to be watered towards the evening. When I was very young, I had my own little watering-can, and my father used to let me help him. The dry, cracked earth around every plant always looked so parched, so thirsty, until my water poured on to it, soaking every root.

'Just the ticket,' my father used to say. 'Can't you almost feel them flourishing and growing?'

When Jean-Luc kissed me, that was exactly what it felt like: something hard and dry had softened and turned green.

He took both my hands and helped me get off the bed. 'Everyone has been so worried,' he said. 'They thought that . . . I don't know the dreadful things they thought.'

'I do,' I said. 'They thought I was . . . not normal. Mad in some way. I don't know. I think they thought I was hopeless. A hopeless case.'

'Then let us go down. Let us show them that you are again . . . yourself. Have you got a dressing-gown?'

I told him where it was, and he helped me to put it on. Tenderly, like a parent with a small child, he drew my arms through the sleeves, and tied the belt. Then he kneeled down and put on my slippers.

'*Voilà*,' he said proudly. 'Let us go and find your parents.'

Something (the squeak of the window, the whispers in the corridors) must have woken them up. They were standing at the foot of the staircase, looking up at me with tears of happiness in their eyes as Jean-Luc led me down into the hall.

**Loosely based on the tale of *Snow White*,
the Egerton Hall stories continue with**

Pictures
of the
Night

Adèle Geras

Are stepmothers really as wicked as their reputation?

*Is Bella haunted only by her imagination,
or is there something more sinister in the air?*

Only the right person can break the spell.

I used to go to Aladdin's Cave almost every day, partly to see Jeannie and partly because there were always new goodies to be found there, especially in the boxes set out on trestle tables on the pavement outside the shop, where nothing cost more than a shilling. Greg usually came with me, but yesterday I was alone in the house.

'I don't like leaving you all on your own here,' Greg said.

'No one even knows I'm here. Anyway, I thought I'd go down to Jeannie's shop for a while.'

'Don't be long then,' Greg said. 'And make sure you lock the door behind you when you get back.'

'You sound like my dad,' I told him. 'I'll be fine.'

And I was fine. I set out for Aladdin's Cave feeling very cheerful, and began rummaging happily through the shilling boxes as soon as I'd said hello to Jeannie.

I didn't really pay much attention to the woman who passed close beside me to go into the shop. I only noticed, in a half-hearted, absent-minded sort of way, that she smelt very faintly of 'Je Reviens' and that as she passed, a cloud spread itself over the sun and I felt, all at once, quite cold. She was inside the shop with Jeannie for about fifteen minutes and then she left. I got a better look at her this time. What struck me about her was that she appeared faded, as though she were a faint carbon copy of a real person. She wore grey and her hair was grey and she had most of her face hidden in a chiffon scarf. She was carrying a battered brown suitcase, and she walked quickly past me, and down the road. At the time, I could have sworn she didn't even look at me.

'Who's that?' I asked Jeannie.

'One of my suppliers,' Jeannie said. 'No one you'd be interested in. She brings me bits of lace and stuff.'

When I went home, I let myself in with my key, and slammed the door behind me. I forgot to lock it, of course. We all forgot, all the time, and no one ever troubled us. It wasn't as though there was anything worth stealing in the house. I went down to the kitchen to make some tea. I hadn't been there more than five minutes, when I heard someone in the hall.

'Hell-oo,' said an unfamiliar voice. 'Yoo-hoo! Is there any-one at home?'

It was a woman, and she was calling out to me, so I didn't feel at all nervous. She must be a neighbour, I thought, one I haven't met yet. I'd better go and see what she wants.

I walked up to the hall, and the first thing I saw was a white cat. It looked just like Snowflake, the cat I used to have when I was very young, the cat that my stepmother had claimed she was allergic to...I didn't want to be reminded of her, and I wanted this one out of the house. I said:

'Is that your cat?' to the woman who was standing in the shadows by the hatstand, and then I saw she was the one from Jeannie's shop. She even had her brown suitcase at her feet. I looked at the pretty, fluffy creature who by this time had run up a few stairs and was sitting there as though it intended to stay. I said, 'How did you know where I live? Did you follow me? And is that your cat?'

'That's no cat of mine, ducky. I'm what you might call allergic to them. Must have crept in behind me...and yes, dear, I did follow you, cos I saw you at Jeannie's, didn't I, and I says to meself, Em, old girl, that child's a real beauty and if ever you had an ideal customer, she's the one.' The woman took a step forward and patted her suitcase. 'I've got stuff in here, dearie, that'll make your heart beat faster, and that's why I came after you, see? To show you…'

'Why didn't you show this stuff to me, whatever it is, when you noticed me in the shop? I don't like the thought of you following me, I must say.'

'Well, I'm very sorry, I'm sure, miss, but I meant no harm, honest. Only you've got to be a bit smart in my line of work, see. Seize any opportunity that comes along, like. And you being such a pretty girl, I thought: she'll love you for this, Em. She won't be able to resist what you've got to show her.' She patted the brown suitcase encouragingly and smiled.

I have to admit that I was tempted. There seemed to be no actual harm in her, although something in her manner, or her way of smiling, sent a shiver down my spine.

'Well, come in then,' I said reluctantly. 'Come down to the kitchen. I was just making some tea.'

'Oh,' said the woman (Em, she'd called herself). 'I can see that I was right about you, sure enough. Not only beautiful, but kind.'

She pulled a chair up to the table and sat down with her brown suitcase beside her. 'Two sugars, if you don't mind.'

I made the tea. The cat (oh, he did look like Snowflake! Who did he belong to? He wasn't one of the cats I'd seen wandering in the back gardens. I must ask Greg about him) came into the kitchen and jumped on to the windowsill.

All the time we were drinking our tea, the woman babbled on. I felt more and more uncomfortable, because what she was talking about was me, and my looks. She seemed tobe gloating over them, but underneath the praise, the compliments, the extravagant comparisons she kept making between me and every famous beauty you can imagine, I could feel – this is the best way I have of describing it – a thick layer of dislike, of envy and even malice in everything she said. Clouds had massed in the sky and it was getting quite dark in the kitchen. I wanted to go and turn the light on, but to do this, I'd have had to pass Em's chair and this made me hesitate. Suddenly I wanted her gone: out of the house. Something in the way she drank her tea, the way she sat at the table was very familiar. I could hardly see her face in the dim light. I said:

'All my friends will be back in a minute. Don't you think you'd better show me what you've got in your case? That is, after all, why you came, isn't it?'

She stood up. 'It is! Of course it is!' she said. 'May I put my case here on the table?'

'Yes,' I said, 'and could you turn the light on, too, please? The switch is on the wall over there.'

She was obviously cleverer than I realized. She was quite right about the contents of her case. It had in it everything in the world that I most desired: exquisitely beautiful scarves and shawls and fans and jewels. I wanted every single thing. I said:

'You're right. It's all very beautiful, but I can't afford any of this. I haven't much money.'

'Then let me make you a small present,' she said. 'After all, you did invite me in for tea.' She laughed and I thought: I've heard that laugh before somewhere and then the thought left my head like a trail of smoke floating away from a cigarette.

'Oh, no, I couldn't,' I said. 'I couldn't accept a present.'

'I don't see why not,' she said, 'if it pleases me to give you one.' She pulled a wide pink suede belt from the whirlpool of laces and silks that frothed in her case and said:

'Come over here and let's try this for size.'

I went and stood in front of her. I was mesmerized,

fascinated to see how I would look. I was wearing black trousers and a black polo-necked jumper. I stood in front of Em and raised my arms so that she could put the belt round my waist and tie the thongs of fine leather that held the ends together at the back. It seemed to take her rather a long time.

'It's a bit fiddly,' she said, 'this fastening. Good job I'm here to help you, eh?'

'Yes,' I said. 'Thank you very much.'

'Don't thank me, duck. It's made for you, that belt. There's no one else would suit it like you do.'

She left soon after that, and I was glad to close the door on her. I flew upstairs after she'd gone and stood in front of the only mirror in the house (propped up beside the window in Pete's room) to admire myself. I looked wonderful, and went to look out of the window to see if I could still see Em in the road. There she was, down by the corner, looking up at me.

The thought came to me: that could be Marjorie...that's how she walks exactly. Well, I told myself, there's nothing strange about that. People often do resemble one another. I pranced about in front of the mirror for a while, enjoying how tiny my waist looked in my new belt. Then I thought: I'd better take it off, and I pulled it round so that the fastening was now at the front where I could undo it. It was laced up like a shoe, and I began pulling at the ends of the laces, thinking that the knot would fall open at once, but it didn't, and the harder I pulled the tighter the belt became and the angrier I felt. I'd seen a special chair in a museum once, long ago, into which they tied criminals, binding them to the back and arms by an intricate arrangement of leather straps. The more the prisoner struggled, the tighter the bonds grew, until they cut cruelly into flesh. This belt was like that.

'But it can't be,' I said aloud to myself. 'They're only skimpy little laces.' I gave them another tug, and then I found that I could hardly breathe. I knew what I had to do. I had to cut the laces. Pete's house is not a place where you can depend on finding a pair of scissors. I daresay I could have unearthed some if I'd turned the place upside down, but there wasn't time for that. I was beginning to feel faint. I stumbled down the stairs, thinking: I must get to the knives. I can cut the laces with a kitchen knife.

That was the last thought I remember.

Pictures of the Night

ISBN 0-09-940973-9

£4.99